PRAISE FOR
"THORNS" and K.L. YOUNG

"K.L. Young's **Thorns** is an immense pleasure to read despite - or because of - the impending sense of doom that begins on the first page and doesn't let up until the last one. This is a story of love, grief, and obsession, a terrible and unrelenting combination that blends deep character study with psychological horror and supernatural dread. It's not just a ghost story with one gutpunch after another; it's a haunting portrayal of love, loss, and the lengths we'll go to keep the past alive - even when it refuses to stay buried. If you love horror that gets under your skin and lingers in your mind long after you close the book, don't miss this one."

- **Ryan Rennik,**
  Author of Black Site, Black Mother

"Can't wait to see more from K.L. Young."

- **Mark Rahner,**
  (Rotten, Vampirella, The Twilight Zone)

"This is some beautiful writing."

- **S.P. Miskowski.**
  Author of The Worst Is Yet To Come
  and I Wish I Was Like You

"K.L. Young is a writer to watch."

- **Hellnotes**

THORNS

STRANGE
AEONS

THORNS

K.L. YOUNG

Also written by K.L. Young

The Secret Language of Spiders

<u>chapbooks</u>

The Ballad of Erik Zann
(Illustrated by Rob Corless)

Infernal Combustion
(Illustrated by Ben '1314' Hansen)

Shaine The Hellslinger
(Illustrated by Rob Corless)

Anno Carcosa:
One Year Under Twin Suns
(Illustrated by Rob Corless)

<u>novellas</u>

Widowed
A Distant Silver Melody

available at
www.writtenbyklyoung.com

STRANGE AEONS

-2025-

© K.L. Young
Cover and interior art © Wade Chitwood

This book is a work of fiction. Names,
characters, places, and incidents are either a product
of the author's imagination or used fictitiously and any
resemblance to persons living, dead, or reanimated in
the form of a shrubbery is purely
coincidental.

Strange Aeons LLC
Seattle, WA
USA

www.strangeaeons.net

ISBN: 978-0-9817503-2-3

as always,
for babydoll

PART ONE

PROPAGATION

NO ROSE WITHOUT THE THORN

"Life is like a rose, beautiful and often surprisingly painful, but there's not one without the other. The two are inseparable, aren't they? Beauty and pain, forever intertwined. The people we meet come into our lives like **thorns**, marking us in ways shallow and occasionally very deep. The thorns shape us, sometimes in the most difficult of ways."

- Charles Perry,
No Rose Without the Thorn

1

"We've slept too long."

It was just a whisper, but it launched Samantha from her bed like a shotgun blast. Eyes wide, breath hitching, she wiped hot tears from her cheeks and turned to Charlie's side of the bed.

Empty, of course. Utterly bare. She'd bought a new bed more than a year ago, but hadn't been able to bring herself to place a pillow on his side yet.

It had been months since she'd had that particular nightmare, and it took a moment for her heart to stop thudding against her sternum. Early morning sunlight crept through the edges of the blinds, bright and hot already, revealing taped up moving boxes and the items she still needed to pack. Books and knickknacks, mostly. Nothing important. The darkroom chemicals and supplies had been boxed for a month, but she'd delayed packing her cameras and lights, kidding herself that she might start using them again any time soon. They'd be the last to be loaded, she knew that much.

A groan escaped as she slipped out of bed, shuffling into the bathroom. She tested the shower and stepped into the scalding water without a second thought, hissing and embracing the burn. The water cascaded over her head, and she vowed to herself if she didn't find the perfect place today, she'd just choose randomly from the eight she'd already seen this month. Moving back to Seattle would make the most sense if she were actually concerned about continuing her photography business, but it was the last thing on her mind anymore, and she'd grown to love the small town of Heather. It easily earned the title of the most charming of the three tiny cities that locals referred to as The Treble, which included Heather and its neighboring towns, Sunset and Kobbe's End; and property values – high throughout Washington – were still considerably cheaper on the eastern half.

The condo sat just off downtown Heather's Main Street, and Sam sat at the driveway entrance for a few minutes, waiting for a break in the passing traffic.

She and Charlie had spent a romantic weekend in Heather seven years earlier, and the tiny town had charmed them so much they used their last evening there searching local property listings.

Houses were hard to come by, but condos were plentiful and they were moved in within three months. Since then, Heather had been named

"Friendliest Small Town in America," and the population had nearly doubled.

The increase ushered in taller buildings and wider roads, and these days it was not uncommon for a ten minute walk to take thirty or even forty minutes by car, due to the unending construction.

When she finally jerked her Outback out of the driveway and into town, Sam snickered at the statue that dominated the center of the main traffic circle. It was local boy done good, Erik Zann, an 80's rock god who had died tragically in a concert fire that claimed the lives of many of his fans as well.

The statue depicted the young rocker in his signature stage pose, bent backwards at an angle that defied gravity, guitar held high, fingers flying across the fret, and Samatha recalled how Charlie would grumble every time they drove past it. He'd felt the monument was ground zero for the annoying growth spurt that occurred in Heather after it was built.

Charlie had attended the town's planning meetings before the statue was constructed, complaining it would bring more tourists to the downtown area, creating even more traffic.

That had been the plan, of course, and now the five streets that spread from Zann's monument like spokes from a wheel were populated with art galleries, wine tasting rooms, and amazing restaurants. Even Charlie had to admit that the modest downtown area had become a local delight.

Leaving the tourist district brought Sam to old Heather, a suburban area full of big, old country plats that hadn't been gentrified yet, and she liked the idea of getting away from the construction signs, cones, and flashing lights.

The homes here were large, with huge lawns; and the occasional business, mostly landscaping companies, dotted the area. She passed a Williford's Supermarket and even one of the last Morgret & Sons hardware stores.

There was no traffic as she turned onto the block the property was listed on, and she parked the Outback in front of the hand made "For Rent" sign at the end of the street, taking in what she could see of the house. It was a late '60s modernist two-story, surrounded by an old, peeling wooden fence. It looked like it might even have a small backyard.

The street ended at an overgrown vacant lot which bordered one side of the house. A neighboring house stood just a little too close for comfort on the other side.

There was something about the place that immediately struck Sam, a quirky vibe she couldn't quite nail down. She liked the peeling fence, and she liked the long grass of the vacant lot on the side. The driveway was asphalt, buckled and cracked, but that also appealed to her today. Charlie's influence, she was sure. This was the kind of place they had searched for before they settled on the downtown condo.

This is the one, she thought. *As long as it has a decent washer and dryer, this is the place. The rent is more than reasonable.*

The front door opened, and an older woman in a dark sundress leaned out and waved at her. She was pretty in a granola-hippie, Diane Keaton kind of way, and Sam put on her best smile as she got out of the Subie, lifting her own hand in return.

"You must be Samantha," the woman said, flashing unnaturally white teeth and extending a weathered hand as she approached.

Sam gripped the hand and gave it a firm shake. "I am," she said. "Sam is just fine. You must be Kim. Very nice to meet you."

"Come on in," Kim said, holding the front door open.

Sam smiled as she entered, noting the scarred wood floors and bold crown molding.

Oh my God, came Charlie's voice in her head, and she thrilled to hear it after such a long absence. *This place is GROOVY.*

She smiled. *Of course you'd think that. Not everyone has your love for modernism and brutalism.* She almost groaned at the sudden, physical ache in her chest. These were descriptors she never would have used before Charlie had introduced them to her.

But everyone should, he said, and she could almost hear his chuckle.

"So, the place has been vacant for years," Kim said cheerfully, breaking the spell and walking them through the spacious, empty living room. "But I've come over occasionally to vacuum and dust."

Off to one side was an entrance to the kitchen and dining area, and to the other, a sturdy, narrow staircase leading to the second floor, the old wood steps covered in a fine layer of dust.

"But not occasionally enough, I guess…"

Sam smiled, motioning to a gigantic bookshelf sitting near the door. "Is that staying?"

"It is if you want it," Kim shrugged. "There's a couple of big pieces that have been in here forever. I should just rent a truck and get rid of it all, but I've been pretty lazy about the place."

Sam cocked an eyebrow and Kim caught it, smiled back.

"I bought the house years ago, after the owners skipped town. I thought I might knock it down, do something with the property. An orchard, maybe." The older woman trailed off, caught in a memory. She saw Sam watching her and finally finished, "And then I didn't. It just never worked out."

"An orchard?" Sam said. "That's different."

"Well, I live next door," Kim explained. "And I thought it might be neat to have a little apple orchard to look out at from the kitchen, you know?"

Sam tried to keep her expression neutral, but Kim caught the changing vibe.

"Don't worry about me living next door," Kim quickly assured her. "I keep to myself. You can do whatever you want here. Have friends over, party it up." She raised her own eyebrow. "You know, reasonably. I'm not a prude, and I'm not going to be over here bothering you."

Sam smiled, but was upset that her emotions sat so close to the surface these days. Eighteen months later and she still hadn't bounced back to who she was before Charlie passed. She wondered if she ever would. "That's fine," she said. "And I'm not exactly a partier."

"I just thought it was time to put the place up for rent. It's been empty for long enough."

They walked into the kitchen, Sam chuckling softly at Charlie's imagined squeal of delight at the sight of the burnt orange countertops and oven range fan shroud.

Over the sink was a single-paned window that looked out over a small, stone patio and an overgrown back yard, and she leaned against the sink to get a better view. "There's a garden," she whispered.

Oh, babydoll, Charlie said. *There's a garden.*

"Just a dirt patch," Kim said, and Sam didn't see the sour look that clouded the woman's face. "Nothing'll grow there. The ground is mostly clay."

The garden was small, just a twelve-by-twelve pea-patch overgrown with blackberries and thistle, knotweed and nettles. On the wood fence behind the garden sat a solitary crow, fat and happy. A small, hand-painted sign jutted from the dirt, listing to one side, its faded lettering difficult to make out.

But not impossible.

It read, *Gwendolyn's Garden.*

They started up the narrow stairway that faced the front door and led to the second floor. At the top of the stairs was a fat, stubby landing, and a hallway with three doors.

"So, what do you do for a living," Kim said, and although the tone was nonchalant, Sam knew when she was being vetted.

"Photographer," she answered, aware of how vague it sounded. She hadn't had a gig in months, and although she had taken a liking to the older woman, she didn't feel yet like she had to explain she was living off Charlie's sizable life insurance payout and the money his discovery continued to bring in.

Kim opened her mouth to say, *oh, that's interesting,* or *what kind of photography?* or maybe *have I seen your work?* and then Sam cut her off.

"This place is huge," she said.

"Almost two thousand square feet," Kim replied, "So not really *huge,* but definitely roomy." She glanced over at Sam. "Not *too* roomy, I hope."

"Not at all," Sam said. "I just can't believe the rent."

Kim shrugged. "I'm doing fine. I don't need the money. I just think it's been empty for long enough. It's time to make someone else mow the lawn."

Sam nodded and smiled, following the woman into the first bedroom. It was large and had an assembled queen-sized bed frame and headboard, with no mattress. An old nightstand and matching dresser were already in place.

"Any of this stuff can be tossed," Kim said. "Say the word and it's off to the dump."

"I kind of like it," Sam said, unsure if that was the truth. She knew Charlie would have loved it, but he had gone silent again. "I can figure it out as I go along."

Kim nodded and they continued the tour, looking into another, smaller bedroom. This room, similar to the others, was sparsely furnished, this time with a single chair and an old, long office desk. Sam's mind wasted no time in transforming the space into a new darkroom. The single window could be easily plugged and ventilated.

Kim patiently waited as the woman evaluated the room, then directed her to what was apparently the house's single bathroom.

Sam couldn't help but smile when she saw the hideous, Pepto Bismol color of the matching sink and tub, although the pink porcelain paint was scarred and scored from the years. She was painfully aware of the absence of Charlie's voice in her head, but he came and went these days, and heartbreakingly less frequently. Each time she wondered if it would be the last. She knew that he would have genuinely loved the colors of the bathroom and the star-patterned linoleum, and that was enough.

"Weird that the only bathroom is on the second floor," she offered, but Kim didn't bite. It didn't matter. She'd only mentioned it in the hopes that Charlie would answer, and when he didn't, the moment was lost.

She didn't notice Kim's growing agitation and the way the woman's eyes kept straying to the old, faded bathtub, hanging there for long moments.

"I love it," Sam said, startling the older woman.

"Oh, good," Kim replied, visibly relieved.

"I *want* it."

Elated, Kim immediately led Sam out of the bathroom and down the stairs. "Let's get the paperwork started!"

After signing the lease and handing over the keys, Kim closed the fence gate between the two properties and walked across the lawn to her own house, feeling better about the neighboring property than she had in years. Samantha exuded kindness, albeit with a hint of sadness, and Kim sensed there was most definitely a story there. But maybe a friendly neighbor living in that house could help Kim reconcile with the memories of all that had happened so many years ago.

₧₨

Two days later, Sam pulled into the buckled driveway of her new home, followed by a "Pete's Moving Service" truck that was carrying boxes full of her worldly possessions.

She'd packed the Subie with her most precious belongings, including the wine glasses Charlie had given her during their early dating days (only two remained after two had shattered in the dishwasher over the years), his books, their wedding photos, and her K-1000. The vintage Pentax was a gift from Charlie when his research started bearing considerable fruit. He'd made it clear that professional documentation was a must, and she was the documentarian of choice.

Strapped into the passenger seat was the subject of that documentation, Blue Charlie, the prize-winning, impossibly blue rose bush that had allowed them such a lavish lifestyle at the end, recently transplanted from the back patio garden at the condo, but looking no less magnificent in his temporary, five-gallon plastic pot.

She unlocked the front door and let the three movers in, one of whom had a ridiculous handlebar mustache and appeared to be the titular Pete. She unpacked the boxes as they brought them into the house and tried not to let Pete's leering gaze get to her.

She finally retreated upstairs after overhearing Pete commenting to one of his workers just a little too loudly about her "spectacular little ass." Her first inclination had been to let him know she was exclusively interested in men who wore shirts that covered their entire belly, but then decided to just ignore it and avoid the movers until they were done.

Mostly she'd been caught off-guard to find that anyone looked at her in any kind of sexual way anymore. She hadn't been interested - or even thought about - sex in the last eighteen months and staring at her reflection in the upstairs bathroom mirror, all she could see were negatives, the gray strands and crow's feet that had appeared since Charlie passed. She was thirty-seven now and could admit to herself that she had kept the weight off, at least - grief was a hell of a diet plan, apparently. She was pretty once, she knew that. Gorgeous, if she were to believe Charlie and his constant compliments. But she just couldn't see it herself anymore and feared she might never again.

When the movers started dragging her box-spring and twisting her new mattress around the corner of the stairwell, she knew they must be close to finishing, and she squeezed past them to pay Pete downstairs and get them out of the place as soon as possible.

She found the man and his mustache coming through the kitchen door, one hand carelessly holding the Pentax's case -

that camera cost more than I'm paying you idiots to move all this stuff

- from her car, the other precariously clutching the thin edge of the five-gallon pot that held her husband's priceless legacy, Blue Charlie.

"Where do you want this," Pete said, all smiles as the pot threatened to slip from his fingers.

"What are you doing?" she shouted, lunging for the pot and roughly snatching it away from him.

Pete acted like she had spit on him. She wished she had.

"What?" he asked. "I'm bringing in the last of your stuff."

She made a quick examination of the plant, making sure nothing had broken. It seemed fine, its celeste blue petals nearly glowing under the kitchen lights. She glared up at the big man. "This was in my car. What are you doing in my car?"

"Jeez, lady," Pete said. "Calm down. I was just grabbing the last few things. We're professionals."

Sam placed the pot on the kitchen counter and snatched the camera case from the big man. "You guys are done here, okay? I can finish myself. What do I owe you?"

After Pete's movers had left, Sam placed the rose pot in the empty kitchen sink, filling a glass of water and dribbling it into the soil covering the root ball.

"There you go, babe." She didn't know if she was talking to Charlie or the rose anymore, and they were both so intricately tangled in her mind now she supposed it didn't really matter.

She sat down at the kitchen table, pushing aside a few stacked boxes of kitchenware and crockery so she had a clear line of sight to Blue Charlie in the sink. In the afternoon light his petals were a gorgeous, impossible sky blue, and she thought about capturing it in a photo.

It seemed like more work than she was ready to do.

She let out a deep sigh. "I'll get you into the garden as soon as possible."

2

Sam was happy with how the bedroom had come together. She'd wrestled her box spring and mattress onto the old bed frame by herself, then fitted her sheets and duvet over it. Straightening up, she stretched a kink out of her back and considered taking that old pink bathtub for a maiden voyage tonight.

She emptied her boxes of clothing, promptly pulling out sweaters, dresses, shirts and slacks, transferring them to hangers in the bedroom's single closet. Occasionally, she would come across a piece of clothing that she couldn't believe she had kept, and those would be thrown into an empty box that she planned to deliver to Goodwill at some point.

Soon the closet was full, and the carpet was littered with empty boxes waiting to be broken down and recycled. She reminded herself to ask Kim when garbage day was.

Tchotchkes covered the top of the dresser - a stuffed tiger from her childhood, a small lamp, a

Bluetooth speaker that was currently playing some of her favorite 80's rock, and a photo of her and Charlie on holiday in Turkey, a working vacation that had sown the literal seeds of Charlie's discovery and their eventual success.

The last box that needed attention was a small hatbox on the bed. It brimmed with trinkets and souvenirs of her and Charlie's early dating life: photos, concert tickets, holiday cards, even Chinese cookie fortunes, and she knew better than to open it right now. That would derail all the momentum she had built up today.

Sliding open the closet door again, she grabbed the hatbox and stood on tiptoes to place it on top of the tall shelf above the closet's hanging rod. It slid in only a few inches and stopped, blocked by something. She gave it a couple of shoves, even moving the box over several inches in either direction, but no dice.

Too short to see what might be foiling her efforts, she reached up on tiptoes again, feeling along the shelf, but she couldn't get her fingers much past the edge.

Determined now, she dragged the wood chair in from the other bedroom over to the closet, then stood on top and peered onto the shelf.

Flush against the back wall of the closet and taking up most of the shelf's real estate was a shallow, rectangular garment box, covered in dust and cobwebs. She grasped it by both ends and ferried it down to the bed, blowing most of the dust off and letting it float to the floor.

Resting the box on the bed, she gently slid its top off.

Her Bluetooth speaker startled her, screeching wildly with static and then falling silent, the battery apparently dead.

She turned her attention back to the box she had opened. "Huh," she said, unimpressed with the contents.

A man's black suit and white shirt, old and unremarkable, took up most of the box's real estate. But sitting on top of the clothing was a scattering of other items.

A few aged photos of a man and a young girl, presumably father and daughter. One showed them at the fair, another at a public gathering of some kind, and here was one of the young girl in a bikini washing an old muscle car. Sam recognized the driveway the car was sitting in, already buckling and cracked in what must have been many years ago. The man was intense and handsome, big but wiry, with thick hair and hard eyes. She watched the daughter grow up in the photos, starting around five years old and ending somewhere in her early teens, lanky but gorgeous.

What a stunner, Sam thought. She was reminded of one her own father's favorite sayings: *Youth is wasted on the young.*

Also inside the box was a baby's pacifier, worn and dirty; and a grimy, naked Barbie doll, her crotch and breasts scribbled over with permanent marker to make a crude bra and panties. It unsettled Samantha, leaving her with a sense of unease she couldn't quite identify. It was just… disturbing.

Wrinkling her nose in distaste, she slid the lid back onto the box and casually tossed the whole thing into the hallway.

That's going right in the garbage.

Grabbing her hatbox full of her own memories, she stepped back onto the chair with it and slid it into place on the closet shelf.

The speaker emitted another sharp crackle of static before blaring an unfamiliar old country song - Don Williams, maybe. One leg of the chair she was standing on abruptly popped like a firecracker, snapping in half and sending her to the floor with a heavy thump.

"Ow!" She glanced around the room, spotting the broken piece of the chair leg. "What the hell!"

She climbed to her feet with a wince and rubbed at her sore hip, deciding it was time to break that bathtub in as soon as possible.

The pink, scratched-up bathtub was smaller than the one in their condo had been, but the water was scalding, just the way Sam liked it. She'd tossed a bath-bomb in and though she couldn't swear by the "healing aroma" the label boasted, it took her mind off her aches as she dunked herself under.

To cool the room down a bit, she cracked the window above the tub. She'd unpacked her regular wine glasses after making sure Charlie's nice glasses had been put away, and sipped from a generously poured glass of cab franc as steam ribboned up around her with the gentle air current. She even brought in a ramekin of frozen Junior Mints, an unorthodox wine pairing she and Charlie had discovered on their single vacation to Walla Walla.

Bobby Darin's "Easy Living" began playing through the speaker, which was working fine again, and now perched on the tub's matching pink sink. She had pulled up an old playlist that Charlie had created some time ago, a collection of jazz and big band torch songs that had grown on her over the years.

The soft music, the wine, the heat, not to mention the stress of moving today - both mental and physical - was all conspiring against her, and she felt her eyelids growing heavy.

But Dean Martin's "Innamorata" followed Darin, and her eyes popped open, her thoughts thrown back to how Charlie would drag her off the couch and make her slow dance in the living room anytime the crooner popped up. He had a passable Dean Martin impression, and he would sing softly to her in a comically drunk baritone as they held onto each other for dear life, swaying to the music.

A gust of cold air through the open window raised pleasant goose flesh on her exposed shoulders. It brought to mind the giant windstorm a few years back that had knocked out power on their block, including their condo building and their favorite restaurant, just past that ridiculous statue in the roundabout. She had just finished dressing to the nines for dinner when the blackout hit, and a quick call confirmed that the restaurant was without power as well.

Seeing how disappointed she was, Charlie had lit candles through the house and cracked a bottle of their favorite Meritage, pulling music up on his ancient Zune, and they started dancing in the living room to The Bill Evans Trio's version of "When I Fall in Love."

The drinking had continued as the storm raged outside, and when the thunder and lightning began, their dancing turned to kissing and groping, and then to desperate lovemaking throughout the house, their clothes tossed willy-nilly as they went from the couch to the kitchen table. It had all ended in a wildly uncharacteristic but unforgettable bout of sex on the outside deck as the rain and wind pelted them and the lightning flashed above.

In the steaming water of the tub, Sam felt herself responding to the memory and dipped a hand between her legs, delicately at first, gauging her commitment to the act, but then with firmer pressure as she remembered how Charlie had looked and felt that night, how primally connected they had been to each other.

He had worshipped her body, and she had reciprocated in an amazing combination of sweet words and filthy deeds, and they had promised each other that their love would last beyond the physical world, through the end of the Universe, and even past whatever came after that.

There it is, she thought as she teetered on the edge, and with that knowledge came a sense of relief that surpassed the pleasure of the impending orgasm. It had been a long goddamned time.

But then:

"We've slept too long."

Water sloshed over the rim of the tub as Sam jerked upright.

"Fuck!"

She yanked the drain plug and stepped out, frustrated, and began angrily drying herself off. In the ten or twelve times she'd attempted to pleasure herself since Charlie had died - mainly because she was bored or couldn't fall asleep - she'd only been successful twice. Her brain - *her arch-fucking-enemy of a brain* - had sabotaged every other attempt, pulling up that last image of Charlie in their bed as she rolled over to nudge him awake.

"We've slept too long," she'd said, poking at him with a smile that faltered as soon as she saw his eyes, wide open and dry and staring at the ceiling.

She'd jolted upright in the bed, her vision suddenly laser-focused, her world shrinking to a pinpoint centered on Charlie. His eyes - always so expressive - flat and lifeless, his lips – the lips she loved to kiss – now parted but drawing no breath, almost blue. His energy had been stolen; his light snuffed. She'd watched him sleep a thousand times since their first night together, and here he was again, just like every morning. And nothing remotely like any morning before.

The love of her life, the most important person in the world, her partner in crime 'til the end of time - her *fucking soulmate*, goddammit - had died at some point in the night, lying right next to her, and she hadn't had the simple courtesy to even notice until morning.

She'd wasted time trying to shake him awake, even slapping his face a couple times, attempting faintly remembered CPR, despairing at the coldness of his lips against hers, knowing this was their last, wretched kiss...

The 9-1-1 operator had kept her on the line, trying to stay positive, but the shift in his tone when

Sam told him that Charlie was cold, that he was *fucking blue* ironically, crushed any hope on the vine.

Sitting on the floor next to the bed, she'd held Charlie's cooling hand until the paramedics arrived. His skin was chapped, the wrinkles in his palm standing out in dry relief that cemented everything, a soul crushing weight that drove home the realism of the moment yet somehow enforced the surrealism of the *event,* because that's what this was, a sudden seismic shift in their goddamned lives when everything was finally going so well, because *why the fuck not?*

And when the paramedics started working on him, she'd almost told them *don't bother, he's gone.* But there was a part of her (a little part of her she'd since grown to hate) that hoped they could somehow perform magic, that they could - against all odds - bring back the dead, and she listened to them work on him for a few agonizing minutes that she'd known even then were just for show.

Because everyone in this room knew that there was no hope for Charlie. He was gone. There was no bringing him back.

But only one person in the room would have to deal with what that meant for the rest of her life.

Samatha's eyes burned as the steam wafted from the bathtub, and she decided just then that finishing that entire bottle of cab franc sounded like a grand fucking plan if she'd ever heard one.

The tub drain gurgled emphatically as the last of the bath water passed through it. And because Sam was tired and sad and angry as she started down the stairs, she did not notice that the last sounds coming from the drain sounded less like dripping water and instead like an urgent and furious voice whispering secrets it probably ought not.

3

The next afternoon, Sam sat on the sofa surveying her new living room. The place was adorable, she had to admit, area rugs scattered over the old wood floor had brought some color into the room, and her furniture fit well into the new space.

At the bottom of the stairs sat a big box of old clothes and knickknacks that needed to be dropped off at the local Goodwill, but that was sometime down the road. She knew there'd be a lot more added to it.

Her gaze fell on the boxes of books that still needed to be unpacked. *No rest for the wicked,* she thought, taking a sip from her wine, and moving over to the enormous bookcase the boxes were stacked in front of.

She set her glass on the nearby side table and opened the first of the boxes, pulling out the books that had been packed like a Tetris game and sliding them onto shelves in a loose grouping of topics. Most of them were non-fiction, studies in gardening and flower breeding, although there were several musical biographies, jazz and big band singers, mostly. There was the occasional novel, all best-sellers and all of them belonging to Samantha. Charlie, as imaginative as he'd been, had little interest in fiction.

She took another pull off her wine glass and reached into the box again, the world screeching to a halt as she saw the cover of the book in her hand.

It was a beautiful photo of Blue Charlie, the rosebush that was sitting in her kitchen sink right now. The title of the book, "*No Rose Without the Thorn*," was intimately familiar to Samantha, as it was a favorite phrase of Charlie's whenever a problem popped up during research. Underneath the title was the author's name, "*Charles Perry*", and under that, "*Author of the New York Times bestseller 'Rockstar Botany'*."

"Ah, shit," she whispered, flipping the book over. The back cover featured a photo of her husband presenting a bloomed blue rose in both hands. She noted her photo credit in the corner and smiled wistfully, remembering vividly how excited they both were while she was shooting the photos for the book that chronicled their trip to Turkey and the near-miraculous discovery of the flower that would soon come to bear Charlie's name.

Her finger traced his chin in the picture, and she could almost remember the feel of his scruff against her shoulder. Before the tears could start again, she reached for her wine glass.

It was not there.

Sure she must have knocked the glass over somehow, she searched the floor under the end table, but no luck. She studied the bookshelves she had been filling, trying to pick out the wine glass, now half-afraid she had managed to trap it behind a row of books, Cask of Amontillado-style. But the glass appeared to have vanished, wine and all.

"What the hell?" Returning to the couch, she retraced her movements. She remembered having a sip here... and then seeing the boxes of books... then getting up and moving over there. She mimed putting the glass down on the table again, and scanned the floor as if she had x-ray vision.

I'm losing my mind, she thought, and then the loud chime of the doorbell shattered her concentration.

Sam opened the front door with some trepidation, unsure who could be knocking on her door already, political pollster or Jehovah's Witness, and instead found Kim, beaming and presenting a large gift basket.

"Hi," the older woman said. "I promise I'm not here to bother you. I just brought a tiny housewarming gift... brownies and wine and cheese and some other stuff to welcome you to your new home!"

Sam smiled and pushed away the twinge of annoyance she felt at the thought of her new landlord visiting so soon. She noticed how nervous the older woman was and felt instantly guilty.

She's trying to be friendly, you asshole.

"Wow," Sam said, accepting the basket, and the two women began talking over each other simultaneously.

"You didn't have to do this-"

"It's no big deal-"

"No this is amazing, and incredibly sweet-"

"I promise I won't bother you anymore."

Sam raised a hand, silencing them both. "Wait," she said. "Did you say wine?"

That elicited a laugh from Kim, and Sam opened the front door wide. "Come on in. I'm in need of wine." She turned back to the living room and her landlord followed her inside.

"Oh my God," Kim said, glancing around the room. "The place looks great!"

Sam smiled at the compliment, pulled the wine out of the basket as she continued into the kitchen. "Thanks," she said over her shoulder. "It really just needed a little TLC." She removed the bottle of wine from the basket. "By the way, we're drinking this *right now.*"

Grabbing a wine glass out of the cupboard, she examined the bottle of wine. It was a generic red blend with a screw top cap. *Beggars can't be choosers,* she thought.

In the living room, Kim laughed. "Well all right, then," she said, sitting on the couch and taking in all the changes Sam had made to the place. She picked up a book with a blue rose on the cover, casually thumbing through it. It seemed to be equal parts gardening and math, way too intellectual for her tastes.

"Do you see a wine glass out there?" Sam called from the kitchen, and Kim put the book down and glanced around the room.

"No…" she said, drawing the vowel out.

"Weird."

Sam returned with two glasses of wine, handing one to Kim.

"Thanks," Kim said. "You know, this was for you. You didn't have to share it with me."

"What," Sam said, taking her own seat in Charlie's old La-Z-Boy, worn and frayed but ridiculously comfy. "I'm going to drink an entire bottle of wine by myself?" She took a sip from her glass, working to keep her face neutral. "Who am I kidding," she said with a sigh. "I'd totally drink it by myself. I mean, holy Hannah, I need a drink or six."

Kim raised her eyebrows and motioned to the much-changed living room. "I don't blame you. I can't believe how great the place looks already. And you did it all by yourself?"

Sam shrugged. "Well, no. The movers did all the heavy lifting. I don't really have anyone else to help with that."

They sat in uncomfortable silence, and each took an awkward sip from their glasses.

"Oh, this is good," Sam said, unsure yet if she meant it.

Kim took the bait, though. "Yeah. Local winery. My favorite." She picked up the book with the blue rose cover and casually waved it. "A little light reading today? You said your husband was some kind of botanist? But I guess you must be into it, too."

Sam smiled. "I guess I am. A little. Mostly I just take the pictures." She motioned to the book in Kim's hand. "That's him."

Her landlord glanced at the book in her hand, turned it over, checking out the man on the back cover. "Him, who?"

"Charlie," Sam said. "My husband."

Kim gawked at the handsome man in the picture. "So… your husband was a botanist. And an author. And a hottie!"

Sam nodded. "He was. Rock star botanist, author of three books on the subject. And definitely a hottie."

Kim took another sip from her glass, noting the look on her tenant's face. "And so now, he's…"

"Dead."

"Ah," Kim said, nodding. "I guess I figured that. I'm sorry."

"Thanks," Sam said. "It's been a year and a half. I'm just finally, you know, *doing* something about it. Getting on with my life, I guess." She downed her nearly full glass of wine in one impressive gulp and stood. "Who wants more wine?"

"Hell yeah," Kim said, grateful for the change of topic and chugging the contents of her own glass. "I have nothing to do tomorrow. The joy of retirement."

Sam brought the bottle of wine into the living room and emptied it into both their glasses.

Kim watched with what she hoped was a neutral expression. "That is an aggressive pour," she said. Her glass was almost overflowing.

"I've been called worse," Sam said, winking over her own over-filled glass.

They laughed and drank, and drank and laughed some more, and finally Kim held her glass up in a formal toast. "To Charlie," she said, and they clinked their glasses together.

"To Charlie," Sam repeated, after a wistful moment. "He was amazing, and brilliant, and beautiful… and a real fucking asshole, sometimes. I'm serious. He could be a real dick. But I really, really, miss him." She dabbed at her traitorous eyes, wet already. "And I'd give anything to have him back. *Anything.* I honestly don't know how I have made it this long without him."

They both took a deep belt from their glasses, and Kim smiled warmly. "I'm so sorry," she said. "Sorry that he's passed, and sorry that I didn't get the chance to meet him. And very sorry for your loss."

Sam exhaled, her lips turning up at the memories. "Oh, God," she said. "Me too. He really was a good guy. And I loved him so goddamned much it hurt. But honestly… we fought. Hard, sometimes. We also loved hard, I suppose."

She took another sip of her wine, studying the dark depths of her glass. "Love shouldn't *be* that hard, you know? Something that beautiful and amazing shouldn't be that painful." Her eyes went far away. "I guess there really is no rose without the thorn."

Kim glanced at the book cover, smiled, and raised her glass again, this time leaning towards Sam until their glasses could touch. "Here's to a painless beauty," she said. And then, with a teasing wink, "Or a beautiful pain, whichever comes first."

Sam snorted and downed her glass, putting on a cheerful face. "More wine!" she said, feeling more than a little tipsy. "And then I want to show you something very, very cool."

"Yay," Kim said, handing Sam her glass. "But I need to use the restroom."

"It's just 'bathroom' in this house, milady. We don't use the word 'restroom'. We're all just commoners, here."

"Shitter," Kim agreed, with a straight face.

"Rude," Sam said, pretending to be offended as Kim headed up the stairs to the bathroom.

Kim finished using the toilet, wiped and flushed, then turned on the faucet to wash her hands. She noted the small, framed photographs of flowers on the walls -

most likely Samantha's own photography

- the nice smelling soap and lotion, and even the tissue box on the back of the toilet, but she resisted the impulse to glance at the old, pink bathtub.

Even when she started hearing the whispering from the drain she refused to acknowledge it, scrubbing her hands in the sink harder and faster under the hot faucet, gritting her teeth against the sound that was building louder and louder, a roar of white noise now that finally culminated in a high-pitched scream and organic *static*, and then immediate, complete silence as soon as Kim shut the faucet off.

She pivoted and faced the tub, expecting the worse... but there was nothing there. Relieved, she released the breath she hadn't realized she'd been holding and reached for the doorknob.

It was locked. Except that the door only had a small locking bolt at eye-level. There was no privacy lock on the old knob. Still, it refused to budge as she tried twisting it this way and that.

The hair on the back of her neck bristled and she felt a suffocating pressure on her chest.

Someone else was in the small bathroom with her.

Terror turned her blood to ice, and she frantically dried her hands on her pants, then returned to rattling the doorknob back and forth.

She refused to look over her shoulder, to even consider whoever was standing behind her, maybe even *beside her, right NEXT to her*, and now she was yanking on the doorknob, the fear rising quickly in her because she didn't have to *wonder* who was in the room with her, she *KNEW* who was in the room with her and she was terrified that any second would bring the touch of a small hand on her shoulder, maybe around her throat, and she could feel the scream building in her already...

And then the doorknob turned, and the door was flung wide, and Kim stumbled into the hallway, catching herself just before she fell.

She risked a quick glance over her shoulder into the bathroom, her face a rictus of fear, certain of what she would see climbing out of the bathtub...

But there was no one there.

Sam took another sip from her glass and considered the wine. *I think I might be starting to like this,* she thought, surprised. The Eastern half of the state boasted numerous remarkable wineries, but she'd never heard of this one.

She'd refilled both of their glasses while Kim was using the bathroom, and pulled Blue Charlie's pot into the living room, ready to show him off and explain what made him so special.

Sam twisted the pot just a hair to show off its best side as Kim came down the stairs, but her smile faltered as she saw the look on her landlord's face.

"Hey," Sam said. "You okay?"

Kim's flustered eyes darted around the room, and Sam finally realized that she was checking to make sure she had everything she came with.

"You know," Kim said, and her voice held none of the charming sarcasm Sam had become accustomed to over the afternoon. "I'm just not feeling very good, all of a sudden. I think I'm going to go home." She attempted a smile. "Too much wine, maybe."

"Oh, no," Sam said, disappointed. "I'm sorry. I was going to show you Blue Charlie."

She motioned to the beautiful blue rose bush in the pot, and Kim gave it a cursory glance, her smile tight.

"It's lovely," the older woman said, then straightened her clothes and made her way to the front door, Sam trailing behind her. "I have to go now. Have a good night."

Sam just watched as Kim let herself out. "Oh," she said. "Okay. Feel better. Thanks for the wine!"

Kim closed the door without another word, leaving Sam confused and alone in the house.

She turned to Blue Charlie with a bewildered smile. "Well, all right. That was weird."

4

The Keurig gurgled and Sam inhaled the smell of coffee filling the kitchen, orange and red in the morning light streaming through the windows.

She'd come downstairs as soon as sunlight began to creep across the front yard. Her sleep had been sporadic, filled with dreams she couldn't quite remember, and when she woke up again at four-fifty-two, she knew there was no more sleep to be had.

Still in her pajamas and robe, she poured herself a mug of coffee and sipped at it, lost in thought, as she stared out the window over the sink. After a moment of daydreaming, her eyes locked on the little, overgrown garden beyond the cracked concrete patio. The sunlight had finally crept over the side fence, illuminating the weeds and blackberries and thistle, transforming the tiny garden into a beautiful tableau of outdoor nature-art.

Sam turned away from the window, glancing at Blue Charlie's pot in the corner.

Charlie's voice murmured in her ear, *Let's rock this joint.*

She stepped onto the patio dressed to work. Besides her grubby gardening clothes, she had donned leather gloves and had her trusty hand clippers, and was dragging a frayed vinyl tarp behind her.

Surveying the mess of the garden in front of her, she carefully formulated a plan of attack, first clipping as many of the dried and dead blackberry stalks as she could and depositing them on the tarp, and then systematically making her way through the small garden, avoiding the stake holding the faded wooden sign.

After an hour of exhausting, dirty work, Sam had knocked most of the blackberries out, and she could feel the scrapes and scratches from the many prickles that had caught on or broken through her denim work shirt.

With a shovel she dug out the thickest of the blackberry knots that were rooted throughout the tiny garden, then raked everything into a sizable pile on the tarp. Finally, she smoothed out the dirt patch she had cleared.

The ground tilled clean and easy, and she saw no evidence of the clay that Kim had warned her of.

Gwendolyn's Garden, Sam thought, pondering the leaning sign. She had already made a replacement, and firmly gripped the stake with both gloved hands, rocking it back and forth, hoping it would break easily. Was Gwendolyn the young girl from the pictures in the garment box? Sam thought she must be.

The ground finally gave up its grip on the on the old post, and as the stake suddenly came free she lost her balance, falling squarely on her ass, still sore from last night's tumble.

There was a loud *CRACK* from the house behind her as she tossed the sign aside, and she stood painfully, her eyes roaming the windows for the source of the sound.

There. The window that sat above the kitchen sink had a long, razor-thin line - visible to her only because of the sunlight gleaming along it - climbing from a bottom corner all the way to the top of the window frame. When she'd pulled the sign out, a loose rock must have flown over and cracked the pane, but there was no discernible point of impact. It seemed more the kind of crack that might happen from too much pressure against the window.

There goes the damage deposit.

She grabbed Blue Charlie's pot and placed it with reverence in the center of the newly cleaned garden, wiping sweat from her brow with a dirty glove. Stepping back, she assessed her placement of the plant.

Moving to her left a few feet and then to the right gave her a little better perspective on the blue rose bush, and she leaned in to adjust the pot minutely, making sure his best side faced the house, then stepped back again to check her placement one last time.

Satisfied, she screwed the pot back and forth into the dirt a little, making a shallow, round impression, then moved it aside and grabbed her shovel. Pushing a foot against the back edge of it, she cut into the dirt digging the hole for Blue Charlie's new home.

The top layer of disturbed dirt dug out easily, but she began to sweat anew as she shoveled out the occasional fist-sized rock and root.

That's it, Charlie said. *Make the hole twice the size of the root ball.*

Sam smiled at the sound of his voice. "I know," she said, continuing to dig.

Excellent. Almost perfect.

"Hmph," she said, grinning. "Almost?"

When the hole was big enough, she kneeled and carefully pulled Blue Charlie out of his pot. She placed the root ball in the hole facing the same direction she had determined earlier, scraping dirt from the sides of the hole and packing it over the exposed roots, mixing it with the additive-rich soil from his pot.

Yep, you got this, Charlie said. *Make sure the roots are splayed out. Don't pack it* too *tight…*

"I know, I *KNOW,*" Sam whispered, and recited his old mantra: "Every living thing needs air to breathe."

Couldn't have said it better myself.

On top of the fence above her, that single fat crow alighted smoothly. It watched her with a tilted head, keeping close tabs on her handiwork.

She flinched as one of Blue Charlie's thick, lower thorns pierced a leather glove. Pulling the glove off revealed a finger smeared with blood, and she popped it in her mouth and sucked at the wound without a second thought.

Ouch, Charlie said. *No rose without the thorn, right babydoll? We all suffer for our love.*

"No rose without the thorn," she repeated, pulling the glove back on again and dragging in the last of the dirt from around the hole. "Now call me 'babydoll' again."

Charlie chuckled, and she could practically feel him coming up behind her and reaching around with both arms to help her pack the last of the dirt on all sides of the rose bush.

You gotta be careful… babydoll… *or you're gonna get a little prick. And we both know…*

So real did he feel behind her that she grinned and leaned her head back against him, finishing the old joke. "I don't like a little prick."

A loud cawing broke her out of her daydream, and she looked up to find that two more crows had joined the original fat one on the fence, all black as midnight and evidently very critical of her lollygagging.

She quickly swiped a dirty glove at her wet eyes and chided the crows. "Oh, stop. I'm just having a little fun."

A sudden memory of a story her father had told her when she was very young flashed in her mind, one of the few pleasant memories she had of the man.

In the story, a young princess had met her Prince Charming, but the girl's wicked stepmother had the prince confined to a tall tower in a far-off land.

The princess ended up in the hands of a horrible man, an evil king of an awful kingdom. When this news reached the captured prince, he of course devised a plan to escape and rescue his love.

Unfortunately, the prince was found out, and his escape plan ended with him plummeting from the tower to his death.

But in the afterlife, the young man pleaded his case of true love to The Queen of the Crows, who was moved by his story and returned the prince to the land of the living, albeit in the form of a flock of crows.

The prince, in his new configuration, was able to slay the evil king (in the process giving birth to the phrase "a murder of crows") and rescue the princess, but there would be no happily ever after for the young lovers. The story ended with the tearful princess cradling the last living crow, which contained the spirit of the young man, and it died in her hands.

Sam's own hands firmly pressed and patted at the dirt surrounding the rose bush, and she stood, one knee popping loudly in protest.

Blue Charlie sat small but ridiculously proud, with his many thorny branches and his single celeste bloom. She felt a warm glow of accomplishment.

But she had one last touch. She'd made a small sign herself to replace the one she'd torn out, and attached it to a garden stake which she now pounded into the dirt next to Blue Charlie. It read, "Charlie's Garden."

Gathering up her garden tools, she waved a hand half-heartedly in the direction of the crows, scattering them loudly into the air.

"Shoo," she said, smiling. "Go on, now!"

She cleansed herself in a cool shower, rinsing off the sweat and dirt. For a moment she swore she heard a voice in her house. *Kim*, was her first white-hot thought, but when she turned the water off, she could hear nothing but the gurgling drain, and she dried off and dressed without the sound repeating.

Energized and inspired by the garden work, Sam stepped into the small, empty bedroom, sizing it up for a home darkroom. The room's single window could be easily vented with a window plug and covered with a heavy blanket.

She knew she could get the window plug delivered overnight, and she still had plenty of developer, stop bath, and fixer.

The enormous old office table occupying the room was big enough to accommodate three developer trays, and the room had plenty of space for hanging drying wires, all of which she already owned. She went downstairs looking for the boxes they were all stored in.

By the time she finished, Sam had worked up enough of a sweat to consider taking another shower. She'd hung drying lines and placed her trays, the chemicals of which fit snugly under the desk.

An old, thick rug under the drying lines would double as protection from any dripping chemicals and also as a stopgap for any light that might intrude from under the bedroom door.

The window she blocked off with a piece of cardboard cut to fit, with space left at the bottom to accommodate the ventilation plug she'd ordered online.

She was exhausted and starving, but she took a moment to appreciate the little darkroom, proud of her accomplishments today.

For dinner she made a little Korean chicken from a recipe Charlie's dad had passed down and paired it with a Counoise she'd picked up with chicken in mind.

And she thought she'd easily fall asleep after such a physical day, but instead she lay awake in bed, her brain deciding to dredge up every single fight or petty argument she and Charlie ever had. She'd see how she could have explained her side of the argument differently, or maybe just changed the inflection of *one* word, just pushing her pride to the side and having an honest conversation. What had she ever achieved through any of those arguments? Only a night alone in bed if the fight had been ugly enough to send Charlie to the couch, followed by an uncomfortable, mutual apology the next day and general weirdness until things finally got back on track.

In her fantasies, she had the strength to tell him how vulnerable she was feeling. She had the wisdom to see how vulnerable he was when he could not verbalize it himself.

They were both reasonable people. A team, Charlie would often say, working towards the shared goal of marital bliss. If at any time during those fights she had simply kissed Charlie, or just told him how much she loved him and how fucking terrified she was of losing him, the fight would have dissolved immediately. Instead, she'd squandered precious time that she could have spent with the love of her life.

When she finally fell asleep, she dreamed of slow dancing with Charlie in the living room of her new house.

5

The next morning, Sam trundled into the kitchen, still dressed in her flannel pajama bottoms and tank top.

Sunlight streamed through the windows, painting the kitchen in warm pink and gold, and for a moment she forgot about everything, the black snakes that roiled inside her head quieted by a moment of peace.

She dropped a single dark roast pod into the Keurig and sat at the kitchen table, trying to hold onto last night's dream even as it slipped further and further away.

Pouring the coffee into an old mug Charlie brought back from one of the many botanical conventions he had spoken at, she returned to the table for her first sip.

Above the sink, the crack along the window caught the sunlight, sending a long, bright reflection across the ceiling, and she frowned.

She stood up and wandered over to the window, taking another sip from her mug as she examined the damage. It made little sense to her.

Was it just the house settling? Just a coincidence that she had been around to observe it? Her gaze climbed the length of the single pane, and she wondered how cold the place would be next winter with these old windows.

Movement on the patio outside caught her attention and her mood plummeted.

The rose bush, Blue Charlie, lay on the concrete of the patio, torn from its home in the tiny dirt garden, its beautiful celeste petals ripped from the stem and scattered in the disturbed soil.

Two crows brazenly strutted through the crime scene, picking up pieces of the broken plant, carrying them for a step or two, and then dropping them again.

Sam cycled through shock, hurt, and fury like a speeding bullet. "God dammit!"

Storming to the back door, she threw it open and charged onto the patio. She flung her mug and its contents at the crows without a second thought. They swiftly took flight but did not go far, one of them observing her from the eaves of the house, the other from the top of the wood fence that surrounded the backyard.

Sam fell to her knees, gathering up the broken stems and petals of Blue Charlie. "No, no, no," she repeated, her eyes filling with tears and spilling down her cheeks.

How could she have been so stupid? Blue had inhabited the tiny private garden positioned directly behind their condo, but that had been designed and constructed by Charlie solely for the rose bush. Sam had never seen a bird or even a bug around the bush! She used the same soil, the same planting technique, everything as Charlie had taught her.

She felt a presence beside her, Charlie kneeling next to her, and she sobbed, the guilt over failing him and allowing his dream to be destroyed just too much to bear right now after all that had happened.

"Hey now," he said, in that gravelly voice she missed so much. "It's not worth all that. I mean… nature can be a real bitch sometimes. She fucked right back with us, didn't she? But look… it wasn't the way you planted him. It was the crows that dug him up."

The tears continued to fall, and the crows above cawed mockingly in response. "Why would they do this," Sam said between sobs. "Crows don't do this! Why would they do this with Blue?"

Charlie's voice was soft and kind. "Who knows? They've never seen a blue rose over here. Maybe they don't like it. Maybe they know he's not supposed to be here. Maybe they're just here to preserve nature's integrity."

Sam swiped fiercely at her eyes. "That's ridiculous," she said, taking deep breaths to chase the tears away. "And I can't just keep him potted in the house! How do I keep him safe?"

Charlie stood, and she looked up at him, at the lopsided grin she couldn't believe she had almost forgotten. His eyes, expressive and so brown they were almost black. At the way he rocked on his heels and held his hands in his pockets when he was feeling smug.

"I could build a cage for him," she whispered, the words painful to her ears. Chicken wire or plastic cages were common with rose gardens, and Charlie had always hated them, had railed against locking beauty away from nature. It was against everything he believed in.

His smile was sad when she looked back up, and new tears sprang to her eyes. "No," she said. "Of course not. But then how can I keep the crows away?'

"I have no idea," he said, eyebrows arching. "How would anyone scare crows away?"

She closed her eyes, wiping at the last of the tears. When she opened them again, Charlie was gone.

With a last baleful glare at the crows, Sam gathered up the rest of Blue Charlie, heedless of the dirt and root ball pressed against her tank top, cradling him as she rushed inside.

She pulled the temporary plastic pot Blue Charlie had been living in out of the garbage can, and delicately placed the tattered rose's root ball into it, carefully covering all of his exposed roots.

Sam was devastated at the sight, the tears threatening again. This was all she had left of Charlie, and she didn't think she could live without it. The clippings were still viable, of course. Christ, she even knew where to find the original bush again if it came to that. But this was *the one.* The only plant they'd been able to sneak into the country. *This was Charlie.*

Fuck, she thought, knowing she wasn't handling her grief well, unable to do anything about it. She was being ridiculous, and as had happened many times in the eighteen months since Charlie had died, she was consumed with guilt over the way she'd acted when his father had passed many years earlier.

He'd been in his late eighties, the age when people are expected to die, but Charlie was blindsided when the man's time had finally come.

Sam was not close with her own parents and couldn't understand the intensity of Charlie's feelings at the time.

But she certainly did now, after suddenly losing him. They swore they'd be together for the rest of their lives. She didn't realize that just meant the rest of *his* life.

The emotions hit her differently each day, and she soon found out the so-called five stages of grief, or seven stages of grief, or *however many stages of grief* was a load of bullshit. Guilt, shock, anger, disbelief… grief showed up in every stage, at any time it damn well wanted, and stayed for however long it wanted.

She poured a trickle of water into the pot from the tap, leaving the bush in the sink, then washed her hands and dressed swiftly, throwing an old Mariners cap over her messy hair.

Sam left the house, still angry, the Subie jerking in protest as she slammed it into gear.

Three crows watched as she departed, perched solemnly on the front yard's short fence.

She drove past both entrances for the Home Depot, the parking lot of which was already full. She'd left the house in sweats and without makeup, something she'd made a deal with herself she would never do. But things were dire today, and not only did she not want to stand in long lines at the big store, she dreaded running into anyone she knew while she looked like this.

Charlie's research and subsequent discovery had made him - and her, to a lesser extent - well known to not only the garden department managers, but the hardcore weekend gardeners as well, and she just wasn't up to dealing with their questions and/or well-wishes.

Several blocks further down the road was one of the last remaining Morgret & Sons hardware stores. She thought there might be one more left in Kobbe's End, but she hadn't visited in years and had heard that the town was nearly deserted now.

The store smelled old and oily, and she beelined directly to the gardening center, where she set to finding the items she had put together on her hastily assembled mental shopping list.

A couple of three-inch diameter garden poles, one of them eight feet long, the other half that, a box of Hefty garbage bags, and then, as a spur of the moment idea, she started looking for anything that might make her scarecrow look just a little more human.

She wasn't sure what to use for the head of the scarecrow. She dismissed creating something from scratch, like stuffing a burlap sack and painting features on it. That was a bridge too far in her current mental state.

And then she saw the end cap of faux-stone face sculpts. Most were life sized masks of bearded satyrs and fertility gods, surrounded by grape leaves and the like.

But there at the bottom lay a solitary, discarded mask. It resembled a theater mask more than anything else, with open eyeholes and a mostly plain face. The only thing mildly remarkable about its features was the quirk at the corner of its lips, a smirk that seemed oddly familiar to her.

Perfect.

She rolled her cart down the aisle towards the registers, the longest of the garden poles jutting from the front of the cart and inviting any other shoppers to a jousting match.

Closer to the registers she found a section of impulse-buy items - chips, candy, cookies, and energy drinks, cheap ear buds, lighters, mosquito repellant and the like.

Sam grabbed an energy drink with a scowl and tossed it into the cart just before she got to the register, where a smiling young man rang up her items. He bagged the soda with the box of garbage bags, then meticulously wrapped the theater mask with paper before placing it in another bag for her to carry.

"Have a great day," he said, and Sam smiled tightly. She appreciated his kindness, but she was on a mission.

Returning home, calmer now but no less determined, she carted in the shopping bags stamped with the M&S hardware logo, lugging the two wooden garden poles, the longest of which was sharpened at one end.

She dropped everything off on the kitchen counter, leaning the two garden poles against the table.

Checking Blue Charlie to make sure his condition hadn't changed set her mind at ease a bit. His trunk was still strong, and though the crows had uprooted him, they hadn't damaged his roots. He would survive this trauma.

She removed the items from her shopping bags: fifty feet of nylon rope and a ball of twine, the box of Hefty garbage bags, and finally, from its own bag and wrapped in paper, the stone garden face sculpture.

Dragging in the donation box she'd filled the other night, she pushed past the knickknacks and trinkets, focusing on the clothing. She pulled out shirts, pants, sweaters, and skirts, but rejected them all, leaving a pile of clothing on the table.

A sudden thought sent her upstairs and she returned with the old garment box she'd found in the bedroom closet. She laid it on one of the kitchen chairs and opened it, nodding in appreciation at the sight of the old black suit.

That'll do just fine.

Using the kitchen table as a workspace, Sam bound the two poles into a large cross with a length of the nylon rope. Charlie had taught her a few knots over the years, but she couldn't remember any of them right now, and so she pulled the loops tight and tied a standard shoelace knot. The poles were solid when she tried to wiggle them.

Then she took the clothes she'd removed from her donation box and began stuffing them into the Hefty bags in small, measured amounts, tying the bags closed at their top and then using the twine to attach the bags to the poles.

In this manner she soon had a solid, humanoid figure, the basis of a decent scarecrow. She turned to the kitchen chair with the garment box.

What the hell?

The box was gone.

A quick scan of the other chairs and the counters revealed the box wasn't even in the kitchen.

I'm losing my mind. She'd had a scary couple months following Charlie's passing where she'd been self-medicating her depression with an uncomfortable amount of alcohol. It hadn't been until she'd discovered she'd had entire, completely forgotten conversations with friends while she was blackout drunk that she'd realized she needed to cut the drinking back.

But she *had* brought the garment box into the kitchen. She was utterly sure of it. And there'd been no booze today.

Yet.

Retracing her steps, she walked the length of the kitchen, then entered the living room. The garment box was sitting on the couch.

No fucking way. I know I put it on the kitchen chair…

She picked up the box and brought it to the kitchen table, pushing back all of the fear and uncertainty that was feeding the roiling snakes in her brain. Pulling the black suit out resulted in scattering the photos and other items on the linoleum of the kitchen floor, but she didn't care.

First the old white shirt was fit over the poles that served as arms, and then buttoned up. The black jacket followed, the scarecrow taking shape as the stuffed Hefty bags filled the arms perfectly.

She gave it a quick once-over, satisfied with her work.

Sam stormed out onto the patio carrying her new creation, dragging it over the concrete and placing it in the tiny plot of soil marked *Charlie's Garden.*

The crows screeched wildly, surprised and immediately unhappy at this new affront.

She slammed the sharpened end of the long garden pole into the dirt, where it caromed off a large, buried stone. Trying again, she slammed it into the soil once more, and then again until it finally seated itself, standing on its own.

The crows shrieked madly and the day suddenly turned dark, cloudy, threatening.

Her eyes darted to all corners of the backyard, looking for anything that could be used as a hammer, finally settling on a broken cinderblock leaning against the back fence.

Striding to it with singular purpose, Sam yanked it from the ground, hefting its weight as she returned to the scarecrow.

The right tool for the right job.

A gust of wind sent leaves flying across the yard and the crows took to the air, soaring above Sam as she set to pounding the top of the thick garden pole with the cinder block.

The first fat drops of rain fell, and she pounded harder, angrier, the cinder block beginning to crack and crumble.

"Get in there, goddamn you!"

At some point the pole hit something solid - another rock, or a root, or bone, perhaps - but the pole was firmly anchored, planted in the garden now.

The sky rumbled angrily, and she glared back at it, tears streaming as the rain began to fall, her emotions mirrored in the drastic change of weather.

"Fuck you!" she yelled at the sky. "You've taken everything from me! You don't get this! Do you hear me? You don't get this!"

She ran back to the house and didn't notice the crow that tried to dive bomb her, although she could still hear their cries over the growling wind.

Entering the house at a jog, she snatched Blue Charlie and his pot from the sink and headed right back out into the storm and the garden.

As she fell to her knees in front of the scarecrow, the sky above opened and the rain began to pour, finally chasing even the crows away with its fury.

But not Sam. She dug her hands into the shallow hole in front of the garden post, pulling out fistfuls of mud that rapidly filled with the torrential rain.

The sky was black and a brilliant bolt of lightning arced across the clouds above her. A thunderous peal immediately followed it, and still Sam dug, her skin ripping and bleeding, her nails cracking and tearing against the rock and the earth.

"You don't get this," she sobbed, furious and embarrassed at all the deals she'd tried to make in the months after Charlie's death. Deals with God, with The Universe, with the Devil even, if she could just have him back, if she could even just go back and appreciate him more when she did have him.

She pulled Blue Charlie from his pot, her skin torn and bleeding from his thorns, and placed the damaged bush in his new hole, haphazardly filling the mud back in and slamming her fists against the ground to pack it solidly.

Finally she stopped, spent, shoulders slumped, soaked, exhausted. The clouds were weeping so hard now that it was impossible to tell where her tears ended and the sky's began.

Sam kneeled in the garden as the deluge pounded down upon her, her muddy, bloody hands limp at her sides as the rain rinsed and washed them clean into the soil of the garden.

Another crack of thunder followed a flash of lightning, startling her back to reality. She stood, slipping and losing her balance in the mud, finally making her way through the downpour and into the house, leaving the back door open.

When she came back out, she was holding the blank, stone garden mask, and she reached up to hang it just above the drenched shirt collar and jacket of her scarecrow. She examined her creation through the pouring rain, adjusted the mask minutely, then returned to the house, pausing to look back again at the garden, at the scarecrow and Blue Charlie almost directly underneath it, at the hand painted sign that read *Charlie's Garden*. And then she closed the door behind her, exhausted.

The world brims with magic. Not the card trick magic of Las Vegas, which is plentiful, of course; and not the enchantment of that first kiss with a destined life partner, which is much less common, but still happens regularly.

But True Magic, Old Magic, terrifying Magic arises in unexpected moments. It can emerge when a violent act occurs at a cursed locale… or from the nexus of profound grief, colliding with the raw elements of nature and death and tears and blood.

Blue Charlie slumped in the mud, tattered and without bloom, but safe for now, guarded, watched over by his new, looming protector.

And the rain continued to pour, cascading down the thorny stems of the bush, soaking into the freshly packed dirt… it flowed deeper, mingling with the rose bush's roots, blending and dancing with Sam's blood and tears and sorrow… and whatever else lay concealed in that sour, tainted earth below.

She felt like a fool. The shower was scalding hot, and the soap and water stung the abrasions crisscrossing her hands. Her fingernails would all need to be cut down to nothing, and two of them had torn to the point that Sam wondered if she should go to the day clinic, but the thought of explaining how the injuries had occurred was mortifying.

Instead, she dried herself off and slathered her fingers with antibiotic ointment, bandaging them tightly.

The rain continued to fall outside as the afternoon turned to evening, pounding against the windows and bringing to mind memories of the sound of the rain on the skylight of the bedroom she'd shared with Charlie. "Skylight music," he'd called it, and she wished more than anything to be tangled up in his arms and listening to that music right now.

The bottle of Meritage she opened was so delicious she decided to pour a second glass, and then another, and then another, and then the bottle was suddenly empty.

A wave of exhaustion crashed over her. She didn't love how much she was drinking. And she didn't love how tired she looked. Or how she felt. She hated being alive and alone, and that was the thought that she took to bed with her, in a bedroom she wasn't familiar with, in a house that did not yet feel like home.

ℬℭ

She could feel his weight on top of her, how hard he was, filling her up as if they were made for each other. She was aware this was a dream, yet was still caught off guard by its lucidity, hovering between wakefulness and the desire to remain submerged within its depths.

They moved together with a deliberate slowness, their bodies finding a perfect rhythm. Her legs instinctively wrapped around his hips as he quickened his pace, driving deeper into her with increasing speed.

Her hands raked across his back, broad and slick, and when she kissed him, she tasted his sweat and smelled herself all over his scruff.

He brought one hand up to her throat, the pressure just enough to make her moan as he continued to pump, and she almost laughed, whispering his name as she climaxed.

PART TWO
BLOOM

NO ROSE WITHOUT THE THORN

"My grandfather, Howard Loren Perry, had a gift for storytelling. He could weave the most ordinary moments into grand epics, making his life seem like an adventure at every turn. And I, for my part, was a captive audience. I hung on every word—whether it was a love story, a war story, or something more spine-chilling. A particular favorite was the tale of a beautiful blue rose he found while on leave in Turkey. It grew on the outskirts of a small village on the edge of nowhere, and was considered unlucky by the locals, a harbinger of death and misfortune. They treated it like a pest, cutting it out and burning it wherever it popped up. But Grandpa Howard described its color in such detail, I could almost see it myself—this perfect, otherworldly shade of blue that no one else seemed to appreciate. I never forgot that story, not for a moment."

- Charles Perry,
No Rose Without the Thorn

1

Standing at the sink, blowing on the surface of her steaming coffee, Sam stared past the gleaming crack in the kitchen window to the garden outside. Her hair was a rat's nest, her eyes puffy and cried-out. She wore only her robe and the bandages that covered her wrecked fingers.

But none of that mattered right now. She sipped from her mug and contemplated the view.

Blue Charlie, so frail and damaged yesterday, had bounced back.

Astonishingly well.

Impossibly well.

The bush appeared to have grown a full six inches, and several tiny green buds had appeared overnight. The sun's glare on the window was nearly blinding, but it seemed to her the rose's bent stems had straightened, had somehow repaired themselves in a manner that seemed inconceivable.

Above Blue Charlie loomed his new bodyguard, the scarecrow she'd built in a frenzy, the details of which she could scarcely remember. The black suit, soaked from last night's downpour, steamed in the morning sunlight, and the accidental angle of the loosely hung mask positioned its eyes directly at the kitchen window. The mask's smirk seemed to be directed at Sam as she sipped from her steaming mug. It reminded her of the look Charlie would give her when she didn't understand one of his stupid jokes.

Somewhere in the distance the caw of an angry crow floated on the breeze, but the scarecrow was doing his job - there wasn't a bird in sight.

As Sam took another sip, the doorbell chimed, jolting her from her contemplation. She glanced at the digital readout of the old stove. 9:29.

"No way," she muttered, annoyed.

Making her way to the front door, she opened it a crack, expecting a salesman or, less unwelcome, cookie-selling Girl Scouts.

A sliver of Kim smiled through the thin opening, holding up another cheaply woven basket. "Heyyy," she said, grinning cheekily. "Gift basket!"

"Heyyy," Sam said, unable to match Kim's enthusiasm. She opened the door wide, accepting the basket. "You didn't have to do this. Again."

Kim let herself in and Sam glanced through the basket. Some adorable tea towels, tea lights, soaps, and skin lotions.

"And where's the wine?" Sam asked.

Kim grinned, and Sam found it impossible to be angry with her.

"Also," Sam said with a thin smile, "Remember when you said not to worry about you living next door?"

"Did I say that?" Kim asked, mock-chagrined. "Shit."

Sam led them into the kitchen. She put the basket on the counter, pulled a second coffee mug from the cupboard. "Coffee?"

"I've already had my limit for today," Kim said. "So, sure."

Sam raised her eyes to the ceiling, a troubled look crossing her face. "Kim never asks for a second cup of coffee at home..." she said, earning a chuckle from her landlord.

She filled Kim's mug with the same dark roast she'd started the morning with and handed it to the older woman. Kim cradled the warm mug in both hands, noting Sam's bandaged fingers.

"What'd you do to your hands?"

Sam rolled her eyes. "Oh God," she said, embarrassed. She examined her bandaged fingers. "Had a nervous fucking breakdown, apparently. Also, fuck all these crows."

That raised Kim's eyebrow. "Okay... are you fist fighting crows? Because you got to be careful! They're mean as fuck. I saw a documentary. Did you know they'll have sex with other dead crows?"

It was Sam's turn to be nonplussed. "No," she said, "Also, gross. But I do know that the little fuckers tore up Charlie's rose bush."

Kim glanced through the kitchen window, noting the crack that ran its length with a quizzical expression. She focused on the garden outside with surprise that shifted into unpleasantness.

"Oh," she said. "Oh, wow. That's not creepy at all, is it."

Sam joined her at the window, staring out at the scarecrow. "Is it?" she asked. "I kind of love it. Also, the window just cracked on its own. I swear I didn't do that."

"It's an old place," Kim shrugged. "And it's been colder than a witch's tit in November in here. The temperature change could have done it." She switched her attention back outside again. "You really cleaned the shit out of that garden, didn't you."

"Yeah," Sam said, still processing the temperature of tits, witches' or otherwise. "Got inspired, I suppose. Pulled the weeds and as much of the blackberries as I could. Planted Blue, there. And those bastard crows tore him all apart.

"Really? That's weird. I wonder why they did that?"

"I don't know. Maybe the color."

Kim took a sip from her coffee, blew on it to cool it, then looked up at Sam. "The color," she said. "Of what? The roses?"

Sam's eyebrows danced as she took a drink from her own mug. Finally, she could show off.

"Yes," she said. "Blue. I tried to show him to you the other night."

Kim blanched. "Ugh," she groaned. "The other night. I am so sorry about that. I suck."

Sam shook her head. "Not at all. Shit happens. I get it."

Kim smiled. "So," she said. "Blue. I don't see any blue."

Sam sighed. "Yeah. There *was* blue. But the crows tore him apart."

"Wow. That's terrible. I'm not sure I've seen blue roses before."

Sam couldn't hide her pride. "You haven't," she said with a grin.

Kim waited.

"I mean," Sam continued, "You haven't *really* seen a blue rose. It's a color that doesn't occur in nature. Any blue roses you do see have been dyed, or genetically faked. A lot of geneticists have tried before… but Charlie discovered a new rose in Turkey. '*Rosa Charlie Caeruleus*'. Blue Charlie."

"Wow," Kim said, suitably impressed. "That's… actually really cool."

"Yeah," Sam said, and wished more than anything that Charlie was standing there. "It actually really is."

They both stood that way for a moment, continuing to stare at the rose bush and its towering protector.

"Where'd you get the suit?" Kim finally asked.

"Here," Sam said. "In the upstairs closet."

Kim made a sour face. "Really."

"Yeah. Must have belonged to the previous owner."

The older woman stared at it a moment longer, her face unreadable. Finally, she turned to Sam and smiled. "Can I make up for the other night?"

"What?" Samantha asked. "Don't even worry about it."

"No," Kim said, her voice firm. "Please let me. Come over tomorrow night. I'll make dinner. "

"Really, it's not necessary."

"I have wine…" Kim said, letting the sentence hang.

Samantha laughed, then locked serious eyes with her new friend. "What time should I be there?"

Transplanting a potted rose bush into fertile, outdoor soil can offer a deeply gratifying experience. With proper sunlight and regular watering, one can expect vibrant blooms within the year, accompanied by a growth of six or more inches in height.

But Blue Charlie was what you might call *exotic*, and the soil he'd been planted in had been fertilized with pain and suffering, much different than what you would typically find sold in the plastic bags you could find in your local Morgret & Sons.

Throughout the day, sunlight shone down on the rose bush, except for the two hours he sat in the moving shadow of his protector, the scarecrow in the black suit with the quirked smile.

Various crows came and went to and from the wood fence behind the garden, but none made a move towards Blue Charlie.

And Blue himself continued to grow at an alarming rate over the course of the day. Fed by sunlight, the small buds opened and exploded into that impossible celeste blue, even as new buds appeared.

His canes thickened and sported wicked looking thorns that snaked their way up through the legs of the scarecrow's pants, at a rate of speed that most would agree was unnatural, and some might even describe as *supernatural.*

During that time, Samantha busied herself by unpacking more boxes, and if she came across a carton she wasn't ready for, it went right into the spare bedroom's closet.

The window vent and red lightbulbs were installed in the spare bedroom within thirty minutes of their delivery. The darkroom was ready to go. Sam just needed to start taking photos again.

By late afternoon she was back at the sink, washing the last of her dishes and realizing it was past time to change the soaked bandages on her fingers.

Out the window was the rosebush. She marveled at the progress Blue Charlie was making, relieved that she hadn't destroyed her widow's legacy, pleased at her own part in creating the scarecrow that dominated the tiny garden. Even now, he was keeping two large crows away as they sat on the back fence, cawing indignantly.

Her back ached from the arduous work she'd put in yesterday, and she thought wistfully of the shoulder rubs Charlie had been more than willing to administer.

As if she'd manifested it, she felt pressure on her shoulders. Strong hands gripped and began to knead and dig into her aching muscles.

"Oh, babe," she murmured. "That feels good."

There was no answer, of course, but the hands moved down her arms, pressing and squeezing her biceps, drawn like magnets to each worn out muscle as they went.

She put down the mug she was rinsing, surrendering to the massage, and the ethereal hands moved down to her wrists, and then unexpectedly to her hips.

A groan escaped her as the fingers dug in, more than just a massage now as the hands made their way back up her body, finally cupping her breasts.

Outside, the crows started shrieking in earnest, but Samantha was lost in the moment and did not notice.

She pressed her ass against the presence behind her, grinding her hips as the hand, warm and soft, slipped down her stomach and then beneath the waist of her jeans.

"Oh, God," she moaned, then gasped as a finger slid inside of her, and she began grinding against the pressure, her eyes closed, unaware that another crow had landed on the fence outside, and then another and another, all cawing riotously, alarmed, unhappy.

"Yes," Sam whispered, "Yes… Baby, I've missed you…"

Closer and closer, she was almost there. The finger inside of her was quickening its pace, and the other hand had slid to her throat, a new kink she was unfamiliar with, but which unexpectedly aroused her so much that the kitchen lighting, bathed in afternoon reds and oranges only a moment earlier, now took on a seductive and dangerously alluring velvet blue.

She was so fucking close, about to hit critical mass, and this orgasm promised to be a real knee-shaker…

And then out of nowhere came the sound of shattering glass, and Samantha's eyes snapped open, the moment lost. Startled and embarrassed at her behavior, she was sure in that instant that someone had entered her house and caught her fantasizing in the kitchen.

What she saw was a doggy print that had fallen to the kitchen floor behind her, its frame broken, glass shattered and scattered.

"Fuck," she said, wiping at frustrated tears, and for an instant she thought she heard a floorboard creak… but there was no one there.

She was as alone as ever.

The crows continued to go crazy outside, arguing with each other now, as frustrated as she was, perhaps because beneath them, that weird, unnatural rose bush continued to grow.

∞○∞

The first thing Sam noticed about Kim's house was how cluttered it was, while still somehow remaining adorably cozy. The place was goofy and lived in and full of, well, shit. Knickknacks, art, mismatched furniture covered in soft, velvety throws and blankets. And pillows. So many pillows. Kim was clearly an individual with a plethora of interests, all of them colliding in the cultural blender that was her home.

"I hope you like lasagna," Kim said as they entered the kitchen. It was tiny and smelled of cheesy warmth and was decorated in eclectic art prints and featured its own antique rolling wine trolly, which Kim filled two glasses from.

"I love lasagna," Sam smiled.

"Good. Because it's literally the only thing I know how to make."

Sam scrunched her nose skeptically. "Let me get this straight: you can make lasagna, but you can't, say, grill a steak?"

Kim's face showed no emotion. "Nope."

"Macaroni and cheese… from a box."

"Never heard of it."

"Peanut butter and jelly sandwich."

Kim shook her head. "What is that? Is that even words? I don't understand what you're saying." She made sure to enunciate: "LASAGNA. And that's it."

Sam chuckled. "Just gimme more wine."

Kim smiled and refilled both of their glasses.

The night continued with music, and when an old Johnny Kaye song suddenly turned up in the mix, Kim admitted that whenever Greg used to put the song Glasgow Smile on the stereo, she'd known sex was on the agenda. This elicited howls of laughter from Sam as she tried to picture the scene.

When Sam tried to counter with some slow Bobby Darin, Kim said she didn't care for many white singers, which prompted the younger woman to remind her that Johnny Kaye was white. Kim responded to this with an eyeball just hairy enough to make Sam think the woman didn't believe her, and that sent tears rolling down her face as she nearly toppled off the couch from laughing so hard.

Two hours later the kitchen sink was full of dirty dishes, Sam's face ached from smiling so much, and the coffee table had two empty wine bottles on it.

When Sam attempted to pour another glass from one of the bottles, Kim stood up.

"Slow down there, cowgirl," she said. "You're going to ruin your appetite for dessert!"

"You've got to be kidding," Sam groaned. "You might only know how to make one thing, but it was delicious, and I am stuffed."

"We'll see about that," Kim said, weaving slightly unsteadily into the kitchen.

Sam heard the refrigerator open, then Kim returned holding a jar of mayonnaise.

"Yeah," Sam said quickly. "Definitely skipping dessert."

Kim grinned and unscrewed the lid. She pulled out a little baggie of weed.

Sam couldn't hide the shock on her face. "Nope," she said. "No way. Not for me."

Kim scrutinized her openly.

"I mean," Sam backpedaled, "I'm totally cool with you doing it, though."

"What," Kim said. "You got to work tomorrow or something?" Then she narrowed her eyes, suspicious. "You a cop?"

Sam chuckled. "It's just not my thing."

Kim continued studying her. "You know this is legal now, right?"

"Yeah? Then why are you hiding it in a mayonnaise jar?"

"I hide everything in the fridge," Kim explained. "My weed, my passport…"

A bark of laughter burst from Sam. "What? Why hide your passport in the fridge?"

"Duh! If someone breaks into your house, they're not gonna go through the fridge! I hide my cash in the freezer!"

But then Kim took a step back as the realization hit her. "You're a virgin!"

Sam snorted. "'scuze me?"

"Don't deny it! You're a weed virgin!"

"Fine," Sam said, heat climbing up her face. "Yes. I'm a weed virgin. It was never my thing, okay?"

"Oh, we're definitely smoking tonight." Kim's tone was firm. "You don't know that it was never your thing if you've never tried it."

Sam shook her head, more and more uncomfortable. "Really, Kim. I don't want to."

But the older woman was already masterfully rolling a joint. "That's obvious," she said. "Doesn't matter. I was the queen of peer pressure in high school." Her hands kept working, but her eyes found Sam's as she licked the edge of the paper to seal it. "Don't challenge me," she said, in a mock demon voice.

Sam fidgeted, anxious and unhappy.

Kim softened her approach. "It's perfectly safe. It's legal, girl. It's certainly better for you than alcohol, and you've had no problem pounding back a shocking amount of that tonight."

Christ, Sam thought. *She really* is *the queen of peer pressure!*

Her shoulders slumped and she put up one last defense. "I don't like the smell."

"I do not blame you," Kim said. "It's pretty skunky. Now quit being a pussy."

She lit the joint and took a couple deep drags from it before handing it over.

Sam reluctantly accepted it, holding it delicately between her fingers.

Kim exhaled an enormous cloud of smoke and motioned for Samantha to go ahead.

Still holding the joint clumsily, Sam brought it to her mouth and took a tiny puff, blowing the smoke out immediately.

Kim's horror was evident. "Oh, for fuck's sake," she said. "What, you've never seen someone smoke before? Maybe you've never seen a movie? Charlie didn't smoke?"

"Charlie?" Sam asked. "Definitely not. He was very anti-drugs."

"Well, thank God! I was beginning to think he was Mister Fucking Perfect!"

Kim took the joint back and demonstrated the proper technique, taking a huge drag which she held for a few seconds before exhaling another huge cloud of smoke, speaking as she did.

"You want to hold the smoke in for a second," she said, voice strained. "Really draw it into the lungs and -"

She began to cough and hack.

"Oh, wow -" Sam said, a little worried.

"Aw, yeah," Kim said, eyes already at half-mast.

She handed the joint back, and Sam examined it, building up her courage. Finally, she took a big puff, holding the smoke in for just a little too long.

"Yeah," Kim said. "There you go. Let it out."

Sam passed the joint back, smiled hesitantly, and then started coughing uncontrollably. "Oh, no..." she said between coughs, trying to draw a breath.

"It's fine," Kim reassured her. "You're supposed to!"

"I can't -" Sam said, overcome by another wave of coughing.

"Yeah!" Kim was delighted. She took another drag from the dwindling joint and attempted to hand it back to Sam, who put both hands up to wave it away, still coughing.

Kim nodded and smiled through the light haze that hung all around them.

They regarded each other solemnly.

"I don't feel anything," Sam finally said.

Kim nodded sagely. "Yeah, that sounds about right."

And that cracked them both up.

Thirty minutes later, Sam *was* feeling something, and after a moment she identified what was so different. She was relaxed. Almost happy. It had been a long time since she'd felt that way.

She beamed and accepted the glass of wine that Kim handed her. "Thank you for tonight," she said. "This is really nice. This is fun. I'd forgotten what it was like to be with other people. Got used to being alone, I guess."

"Turns out this *was* your thing," Kim said, smiling back.

"I guess so…" Sam turned suddenly to face her new friend. "Tell me about your husband."

Kim pursed her lips. "Greg? That piece of shit? He cheated on me more times than I can count. Hit me more than once. And was the worst lay I ever had."

Sam's eyes went wide. "Oh, shit. I'm sorry… I'm-"

"But he had a shitload of money," Kim continued, "So I dealt with his bullshit… until I didn't have to anymore." She glanced up at Sam and then around her lovely, modest home. "I guess it was worth it."

Sam sipped her wine and Kim took the moment to change the subject.

"So," she said. "You've officially started your new life. Got a new place. Made a new friend…"

"A hooligan," Sam interjected, "And clearly a very bad influence."

Kim barreled on. "What's next? New job?"

"Maybe? But no rush. Charlie left me a nice little nest egg, and a lot of opportunities. I'll be able to sell Blue's clippings for an awful lot of money, at least until someone else grows a variant."

Kim nodded, returning to her line of questioning. "… new man?"

Sam blanched at the thought. "God, no. I'm not ready for that."

"How long has it been? Two years?"

"A little less than that, I guess," Sam said. Then murmured, "Eighteen months and eleven days."

"Jesus," Kim exclaimed. "We gotta get you laid. A date, at least."

"Absolutely not. No way. Not interested."

Kim poked at her. "You didn't think you were interested in weed, either!"

Sam chuckled and Kim leaned over, plucked her iPad from the end table, then settled back in, facing the younger woman.

"Let's do this," Kim said, turning the iPad on.

"What are we doing," Sam said, relaxed, smiling.

Kim began typing rapidly with one hand on the iPad's screen. We're setting up your dating profile."

Sam laughed amiably, taking a drink from her wine. "Oh, no we are not."

But Kim's typing never faltered, flawlessly fluid on the touch screen keyboard.

"Name, Samantha Perry," Kim narrated as she typed. "Widowed. Occupation…" Her fingers finally stilled, and she glanced up at Sam, then resumed typing. "Independently wealthy."

Sam laughed and leaned in, understanding the game now.

"Age?" Kim asked.

"Twenty-four," Sam said with a chuckle.

"Forty-six," Kim narrated loudly as her fingers slid across the screen.

"Hey!"

The older woman allowed herself a tiny cackle and continued to type. "Hobbies."

"Hang gliding," Sam said immediately. "Scuba diving. Mountain climbing."

Kim resumed typing. "Klan meetings. Death Metal. Serial Killers."

This cracked them both up, causing Sam to almost spill her wine.

"Oh my God," she said. "You're the worst!"

Kim ignored her. "What I'm looking for in a partner…"

Sam took a drink, reduced to a spectator of her own digital dating profile. "Well," she said. "You tell me."

Kim smiled gleefully, narrating as she typed. "Someone to attend Klan meetings and death metal concerts with. Helping me hide the bodies would be a big plus."

Sam rolled her eyes. "Perfect," she said.

Kim held the iPad up, pointing its camera at the other woman. "Smile," she said.

Sam didn't understand what was happening until she heard the fake, digital "*whirr-click*" of the tablet's camera.

Kim did her best to suppress her giggles at the image on her iPad's screen of Sam, one eye almost closed, the drink in her hand threatening to spill at any moment. It was glorious.

"What!" Sam said, shocked. "Wait, no! Don't take my picture!"

Kim's face was resigned, despondent. "Oh, no," she said, helpless. "It's uploading right now! I wish there was some way to stop it, but it's in the Lord's hands now. Sorry."

She turned off the iPad and set it aside, leaning over to whisper, "Besides, we've got to see the specimen that responds to this profile!"

Sam shook her head, laughing. A horrible dating profile meant nobody would check her out, and she was fine with that. "It doesn't matter," she said. "I'm already cohabitating with the ghost in the house."

Kim sobered up instantly. "What? What do you mean?"

Sam smiled. "Oh, I think I've got a ghost. Maybe Charlie, keeping me on my toes. You know, right after he died I was positive he was keeping tabs on me, making sure I was..."

She finally noticed Kim, stone faced and unsmiling.

"What?" Sam asked, immediately on guard. "What's going on. What haven't you told me?"

Kim sighed, resigned. "Jesus, Samantha. I'm so sorry."

"About what. What haven't you told me?"

The older woman took a gigantic swig of her wine. "I think the place might actually be haunted."

Sam gulped her own wine and settled into the couch, focusing on Kim. "Spill it."

Kim's eyes were wet, shiny. "It's not a cheerful story."

"Welcome to my world. Let's hear it."

Her landlord nodded, studying the wine swirling in her glass. "Twenty-five, thirty years ago. The family that lived next door. The Huxley's. A girl, Gwendolyn. And her father, Eldred."

"Eldred?" Sam asked. "You sure this wasn't the Middle Ages?"

Kim ignored her and continued. "The mother died young. I'm not sure what her story was. Gwen was only about five. We had just moved in."

"You and Greg," Sam offered.

Kim nodded again, her eyes focused decades in the past. They turned hard. "Yeah. Greg. He died five years later. Right after cheating on me with that bartender from the cafe on Hewitt."

Sam could see the pain in her friend's eyes and said nothing, unwilling to derail the story again.

"Things were always weird with Gwendolyn and Eldred," Kim said. "I could tell there was something going on."

"He abused her," Sam said.

Kim looked up with a dark expression, meeting Samantha's eyes.

"Oh no," Sam said, realizing Eldred didn't just abuse Gwendolyn.

"Yeah," Kim murmured, and continued swirling the contents of her glass. "I kept thinking that's what was going on… and I kept not doing anything about it. For years."

She looked up again, almost pleading with Sam. "I mean, what if I was mistaken? What if I called the cops on what I thought was happening, and then I turned out to be completely wrong?"

Sam reached out and took her friend's hand, giving it a comforting squeeze.

"And finally," Kim said, "I called him out on it one day. I saw them in the back yard working on that little garden, and there was absolutely no doubt what was going on."

"Oh God," Sam said, horrified.

"I was in a blind rage," Kim went on. "I marched over there and pounded on the door."

Sam gasped, picturing the man from the photos she had found in the garment box. Big and scary, threatening without trying. She was now sure that man must be Eldred Huxley.

She imagined a much younger, slighter Kim confronting that big, wiry man and she marveled at the balls this woman must have had.

"I told him what I had seen," Kim said, her eyes lost in the past. "I told him I was going to the police. And we got into a huge screaming match right there on the porch."

"Oh my God," Sam said, entranced.

"Yeah," Kim said, and finally looked up at her. "And then he grabbed my arm and he yanked me right into the house."

Sam's eyes were almost as wide as her mouth. "*What?*"

"He did," Kim said, nodding slowly. "And my shirt tore, and he was looking at me… he was looking at my… and I thought, holy shit. He's going to rape me. My next-door neighbor is going to rape me. And then kill me. I was sure of it."

Sam pictured that young woman backed against the corner of the living room of Sam's new home, her shirt torn, her bra exposed. She was terrified for that young girl. "Oh, my God," she said.

Kim was silent for a few minutes, then wiped at a leaky eye and nodded at Sam. "And then suddenly Gwendolyn was there. She clocked Eldred over the head with a baseball bat like she was swinging for the upper deck. Killed him."

The blood drained from Sam's face. "Oh shit."

"She didn't mean to," Kim explained quickly. "She was only trying to save me. But I think she'd had enough of her father's shit. She wasn't going to let him hurt anyone else. Not me, and not her."

"Fuuuuck," Sam exhaled. "How old was she?"

"Must have been about fifteen, I guess."

"And then what?"

Kim shook away the memories, took a deep breath and let it out, collecting herself.

"And then we called the cops," she said. "They came and collected her, you know, took our statements and all of that stuff. CPS stepped in and I lost touch with Gwendolyn. The house went up for sale, and I bought it a year later. I never found out what happened to her."

Sam leaned back into the old couch, shell-shocked. "Jesus."

Kim nodded. "I've never told anyone that story before," she said. "And I'm so sorry. I thought that so much time had passed. But now this… I think there *is* a ghost in your house. And I think it's Eldred Huxley."

"Oh, God," Sam murmured, remembering her kitchen fantasy. "Gross."

"I know. I'm so fucking sorry. I completely understand if you feel like you can't stay in the house anymore."

Sam nodded. "I mean… I don't know. That's a pretty rough history, you know?"

Kim looked profoundly miserable. "I know."

"And you did the right thing," Sam reassured her. "You saved that little girl. You're a fucking superhero!"

Kim hung her head and they sat like that for a few minutes, both of them staring at the contents of their wine glasses.

She glanced up at Sam. "We could smudge the place."

The younger woman looked up, clueless.

Kim was eager. "Yeah! Smudge it! Clean it of negative energy. I did it here after Greg… after he died."

Sam sighed. "I guess…"

Kim heard the doubt in her voice. "Or whatever you want to do, of course. You can stay here tonight, if you don't want to go back. I don't know what's going on over there, what's happening, you know. Are you seeing things happen? You know, ghosty stuff?"

Sam felt the blood rising in her face. She certainly wasn't going to tell this woman that the things happening over there seemed to be very horny, and specifically *Charlie-horny*.

"No," she said. "It's fine. I mean… something weird is definitely going on over there. But I feel like it's… I don't know. Like Charlie is with me. Making sure nothing is going to hurt me."

Kim nodded, hopeful.

"And, dammit," Sam continued, "This is the first time in a long time that I've felt better about my life. I love the house. And I think it loves me."

Kim's eyes were wet again. "It does! And I love you too!"

She leaned over and embraced Sam, and they both laughed.

"Aww!" Sam exclaimed. "I love you back!"

Kim held the embrace long enough that Sam began patting her back as a signal to break.

"How much of this is the weed talking?" Sam asked.

"Ninety-eight percent," Kim replied, refusing to let go.

Their giggles resonated throughout the house.

Sam's dreams that night were frenzied, her arms and legs wrapped around the body on top of her, plunging into her, harder and faster and even deeper, his hands everywhere, squeezing her ass and her breasts, two of his fingers finding her mouth, and she sucked on them as his hips continued to pump. When those fingers slid from her lips, they found her throat again and she could feel the orgasm approaching. It hit hard and she woke, moaning, her body tensed and tight. As the waves subsided, she promptly fell back asleep, sated and finally satisfied.

2

The numbers fluctuate, but it is generally known that anywhere from 30% to 65% of online dating site users are married or in a committed relationship.

Some of those people - predominantly men - have signed up just to look at the pictures. They create fake names and profiles and use them to safely flirt with other users, with no intention of meeting in person.

Some of them - again, mainly men - are using the sites to covertly cheat on their significant others. They will wine and dine their dates in the hopes of ending up in a sexual relationship with their match.

And some people, for example, Terry Logan, use dating sites to brazenly punish their wives or girlfriends. Terry was married to a woman named Michelle, who was – without a doubt - smoking hot, but could also be a real fucking bitch sometimes. Redheads, you know?

When they fought, which was regularly, Michelle would often storm out of the house and find a karaoke joint in Sunset or Kobbe's End, where she'd end up hooking up with some unsuspecting young man and fucking his brains out for a couple of days before heading back home, leaving her victim dazed and broke and wondering where his good time had gone.

It was the height of childishness, as far as Terry was concerned. He considered himself a hopeless romantic, based on the many adventure movies of the '80s and '90s he'd digested. His modus operandi after a big fight was a little different. Terry preferred hitting the dating apps - he had a profile on all of the free ones - to set up a last-minute meet-up, just to show Michelle who was boss.

He'd meet the woman at a decent dinner spot - not too expensive, but definitely none of the chain restaurants - charm the hell out of her at dinner and pay for her meal, and inevitably end up in bed with her. Terry knew he was attractive, and he always targeted slightly older women - they were just so much easier to score with.

Last night, Terry and Michelle had gotten into it good, and it didn't really matter what had started it. It could have been about the bills, Michelle's shoes, or even toast. He'd been craving strange pussy for the last few weeks, so it was time for a fight.

He knew Michelle had headed out to the Hunan Gate or the Mandarin Palace and she'd be gone for a day or two before returning and begging for his forgiveness. So, he jumped on the computer and began swiping right on several new accounts that had just been uploaded.

If you wanted to catch a fish, you had to cast a wide net.

∞∞

Sam woke to warm, orange, morning light streaming through her new bedroom windows.

She vaguely recalled last night's dream, but not so much the evening that led to it. It had been a long time since she'd had a full-on hangover, but she was feeling it this morning. Her head ached and her stomach was already threatening less than good times for the rest of the day.

She surveyed the room, getting her bearings. Everything was where it was supposed to be, but something felt off. Her throat hurt and she could still taste the smoke from last night's weed, and she couldn't remember if she had bothered to brush her teeth before tumbling into bed. To be honest, she didn't exactly remember leaving Kim's house.

But other than that, all was normal. She felt kind of… *good.*

Sliding out of bed, she stretched her back and shoulders, drowsily making her way down the narrow staircase and into the kitchen, which was practically glowing in the sunlight.

After placing the coffee pod in the Keurig, she shuffled to the sink and rinsed out yesterday's mug, blinking the sleep from her eyes.

She glanced over her shoulder at the blank space on the wall that had held the artsy dog print she'd purchased at the Heather Farmer's Market years ago. It had fallen and broken yesterday in the middle of her... *what? Sexual fantasy?* Jesus, that sounded so immature.

But what else was it?

Sam didn't want to think about what else it was, especially if the answer was Eldred Huxley.

She turned back to the sink, drying Charlie's mug. Glancing out the window, she gasped, and the mug slipped from her fingers, falling to the sink and shattering into several pieces.

"Holy shit," she murmured. But not to the shattered mug.

Outside, the sunlight beamed on Blue Charlie and his scarecrow protector. But they had become one and the same, now.

The rose bush, which had somehow tripled its size in the last twenty-four hours, nearly engulfed the scarecrow. Blue's canes - some of them close to two inches thick! - had wound inside and throughout the jacket and trousers of the old black suit. Several gorgeous blue roses had bloomed at his base and sleeve cuffs, even poking out the neck of his white shirt, reminding Sam of the times she'd tucked Charlie's chest hair back into his dress shirts at various events, earning her a grateful smile from him.

Near the top of the massive rose bush, the stone theater mask smirked knowingly at Sam. Dwarfed by all of it at ground level was the tiny sign she'd painted and stuck in the ground.

Charlie's Garden.

It certainly was now. There were thin, bristly vines snaking along the ground at the rose bush's base, reminding her of some of the rambling rock roses she and Charlie had found on that fateful trip to Turkey that had changed their fortune. Following those strange vines had brought them to the hidden valley where they'd discovered the bush that would shortly share his name.

"Magical" was how he'd described it then, the impossible color and size of the bush they had found. She thought he may have been right. The plant was easily as tall as the thousand-year old Rose of Hildesheim, the size and width of a maple tree.

"Uh huh," Sam said out loud, slightly uncomfortable. Had she made a mistake planting the rose bush here? She wondered how big Blue might grow if left alone. "Some weird shit definitely going on here."

Sam hauled over an old, plastic lawn chair, sun-bleached and grimy, and settled in front of Blue Charlie, cradling the Pentax K-1000 in her hands. The temperature in the back yard was rising, the light changing quickly, and she adjusted her f-stop accordingly, snapping off a few shots, the power winder *whirring* softly as she marveled at the size of the bush and how it had formed itself into a shape that looked like nothing so much as wood musculature through the scarecrow's clothes.

Behind the big bush, five crows perched on the back fence, their bodies negative space in the sunlight, tiny, feathered voids. They scrutinized her closely with their shiny black eyes, but remained quiet.

For now.

"Hey, Charlie," she whispered, taking another shot. >*click-whirr*<

She'd always referred to the rose bush as *Blue* to avoid confusion, but today, right now, *Charlie* seemed appropriate. It felt right. "How you doing?"

The crows shuffled a bit behind the scarecrow as she spoke, but they kept their silence.

"You look fucking great," she continued. >*click-whirr*<

"I mean, not as great as you did when you were flesh and blood, and, you know, *human*, but you've got to be pretty proud of yourself right now, huh?"

The angle of the mask made it seem like it had asked a question of her. She sighted through the viewfinder, entranced by the morning light and shade on the mask. "Me? Oh, I'm *fanfuckingtastic*. I drink too much, and I cry myself to sleep most nights, but other than that, I'm doing great. But I could sure use muchas smooches right now."

>*click-whirr*<

She made another adjustment to the aperture and gestured to the freakishly large bush in front of her. "Blue's doing amazing, as you can see. It was touch and go for a minute but look at you now. I mean... yeah. This is bonkers. Do I have you to thank for this? Or is this just his regular growth pattern? I mean... what the fuck have we done?" The memory of the locals' displeasure with the rosebush resurfaced in her mind, but she quickly shoved it aside.

"I guess you know that Eric and Rick are going crazy at Arkham Flowers. They're offering enough for clippings that I can relax about work for the next year or so, if I go exclusive with them."

And these photos will absolutely seal the deal, she thought. Charlie could have gone with anyone after he had patented the rose - the phone calls and emails had started almost immediately. But the East Coast owners of Arkham Flowers had been so damn charming throughout the inquiry process that there had never been any doubt in their minds.

"And my new landlord is a hoot. Kim. You'd love her. She's old and cranky, just like you are."

Her throat tightened.

Like you were.

The camera *clicked*, *whirred*, and then she heard the flapping sound of the end of the film roll.

One crow cawed suddenly, upset at her constant chatter. She gave it the stink-eye.

"All right, all right. Calm down. I'm done."

∽∾

Sam had forgotten how much she loved the smell of stop-bath and fixer. Well, not the *smell*, which was fucking awful, but the memories it triggered. Good times. Successful times. She'd been well on her way to becoming a top landscape photographer when she'd bumped into Charlie Perry at a mutual friends' party in Sammamish and was immediately smitten.

They'd talked most of the night away there, and then went back to her place and fucked away the rest of it. He proposed to her three months later, and they'd been inseparable ever after, her talents merging with his to lift them both up to become a weird Morticia and Gomez Addams of the floral world that made most of their peers an equal mix of jealous and uncomfortable.

Sam switched out the spare bedroom's regular light for the deep red bulb, then turned on her new window vent and poured and mixed the chemicals, her nose burning at the sulphur and citrus odor.

Winding the film reel in her changing bag was muscle memory, and it quickly came back to her after nearly two years of not developing her own photographs. She tried not to think about what else might be on the roll of film that she'd pulled from the Pentax. It hadn't been used since Charlie had passed.

Would a photo of Charlie send her reeling into a dark pit of despair? Maybe.

But she didn't care. Right now she was desperate for any new bit of him she could get. Her heart positively thrilled for it.

She forced herself to finish developing the film with detached professionalism, rinsing the tank with multiple pitchers of water before finally opening the lid and rinsing the film off directly.

Clipping one end of the roll on her dry wire, she unspooled the film, letting it drip to the old rug below it.

She pulled the blanket away from the window and extracted her loupe. The daylight shone through the photo reel, casting brilliant colors and shapes over her face.

Here at the new end of the roll was the scarecrow she'd fashioned in the suit from the garment box and the mask from Morgret & Sons, and in front of those pictures was Blue Charlie underneath the scarecrow, his impossible, sky-blue color absolutely radiant in the early morning sunlight. And then in front of those photos…

"Oh, babe…" She angled the loupe for tighter detail, focusing on Charlie's crooked smile and his messy hair, and those dark eyes that nearly leapt out at her.

She'd surprised him, it seemed in this photo, and she suddenly recalled the moment. They were in a swanky bar in downtown Seattle, Purple maybe, a late night after a particularly grueling convention schedule.

Charlie, high on the success of his conference speech, just finished ordering their wine at the bar. He was glowing, and she'd snapped the photo just as he was turning back to her.

"Fuck," she whispered, blinking back tears. The photos on the roll in front of that one were also of Charlie, but from a distance as he stood at the podium, discussing his breakthrough discovery to a packed room. There was a photo of Blue Charlie on the screen behind him.

I took these photos a thousand years ago.

She froze at the first photo on the roll and a sob escaped her. It was a selfie of her and Charlie, clumsy in its composition due to the weight of the camera and its power winder, but it had an energy about it, a beauty in its candidness.

She had her cheek pressed up against Charlie's scruff and they were both mid-laugh, their eyes shining brightly.

Sam stared at the photo until the tears blurred her vision, and she slumped to the floor, head between her knees, the tears flowing freely. Not the painful, wracking sobs she had endured during the first weeks following Charlie's death, but the quiet, burning tears that come with horrible, inevitable acceptance.

"I wasn't ready for this kind of change," she whispered through choked breaths. "Not this much, and not this way. It was too quick. You didn't give me time to prepare. If I had known that was the last time we'd kiss, I would have really laid one on you, right? Our last 'I love you's should have been while we were gazing into each other's eyes, not tossed out while we were half asleep."

She wiped at her wet cheeks. "I've tried everything," she said. "I've made every deal with every fucking higher power I can think of, and you're still gone. I guess it's time to think about-"

The doorbell chimed from downstairs, and Sam sprang up, drying her eyes, angry and embarrassed. "Oh, God," she said. "What now?"

She expected to see Kim when she opened the door and she was not disappointed.

Her landlord was excited and a little too put-together for this early in the morning. She was gripping her iPad with absolute glee.

"Kim," Sam said. "It is way too early for this." She noted the lack of a gift basket this time. "And where's my basket?"

She turned and shuffled back to the kitchen and Kim invited herself in, closing the door behind her.

"We got a hit!" Kim said eagerly.

Sam grabbed another mug from the cupboard, filled it with coffee. "A hit?"

"A hit," Kim repeated. "A fish! A dude!"

Sam placed the steaming mug in front of her guest, still oblivious to whatever Kim was trying to tell her.

"A date," Kim explained. "From last night."

Sam wiped at her eyes, annoyed. "You came over to tell me this?"

Kim barreled on without noticing. She swiped at the tablet screen and pulled up the site.

"He's cute," Kim said. "And he's got a good sense of humor. I mean, he gets the joke. I think. His name is Terry."

She flipped the screen towards her friend to show the man's profile, but Sam was not interested.

"No," Sam said.

"Come on," Kim cajoled. "Terrrrrry."

"No way. Not a chance."

"He's cute!"

"I don't care. I'm not interested."

"I already swiped right," Kim said, only a little embarrassed.

"You what!?"

"It was an accident," Kim explained. "I was trying to wipe a little peanut butter off the screen!"

3

Sam found parking close to the tiny Italian restaurant that she and Terry had agreed upon. She couldn't believe she was going through with the date, but Kim had laid it on thick, promising her she'd "have a wonderful time" and that "it was only dinner," and insisting "it was crucial for her healing process."

Christ, Sam thought. *Kim had come by her "Peer Pressure Queen" title honestly.*

She had to admit that she'd enjoyed dressing halfway nice again, and examining herself in the bathroom mirror after putting on her makeup gave her a boost of much needed confidence. And made her smile. Until she'd applied the lip gloss.

That brought back aching memories of how goofy Charlie would act when he saw her applying anything to her lips, and she hastily wiped the shine off. Tears threatened to upset her eyeliner, but she held them back. She'd made herself feel better by setting her hair with a ridiculous amount of hairspray.

Kim had seen the doubt on Sam's face when she emerged from the bathroom and swiftly shifted into cheerleader mode, boosting her up and up, escorting and nearly forcing her out to the car and making her promise to call when she got home.

For a moment, Sam had considered bailing on the date and just going out to one of the old bars she and Charlie had frequented, but thought that might bring her down even further.

She decided she'd go through with it. The guy's pictures were good, and he seemed nice enough. Besides, it was only dinner.

How bad could it be?

The restaurant was dark and cozy, and when Sam entered, she heard Frank Sinatra on the speakers. Terry was charming and attractive, although not at all her type.

Christ, do you even have a "type" after you've been with the same person for seven years?

When she walked in, he was already seated at the table, dressed in a blazer and jeans. A bottle of Syrah was open.

They made small talk as they sipped their wine, and Sam found herself warming to the man. He was lower management at one of the many aerospace businesses in the state, his company specializing in cockpit instrumentation.

Before long, their server arrived and they both ordered the pasta puttanesca, the conversation continuing smoothly over dinner salads as they discussed photography, music, and movies.

Terry took a sip from the Syrah and said, "I have to admit, I expected you to be older."

Sam's eyes widened, and she froze mid-chew.

"I mean," he continued, "Unless you really are forty-six, and just very well-preserved."

Sam swallowed and laughed, finally understanding. "Ah, yes. The dating profile. Well, everyone lies on those things, right?"

"Sure," Terry said. "They rarely add a decade to their age, though."

"That was all Kim," Sam said. "I'm afraid we were in the middle of a girl's night when she created the profile."

"Ah, okay," Terry said. "Is Kim your roommate?"

"Oh God, no. My landlord. And good friend, I suppose."

"Excellent," Terry said. "Good."

Sam registered his reply just a hair too late. *Good? What does that mean?*

And then the server arrived with their dinners, dropping off two plates of pasta that smelled so good Sam's stomach audibly growled.

"Is there anything else I can bring you?" the server asked, smiling.

Terry dismissed him with a wave, and Sam frowned. Charlie had taught her to watch how people treated waitstaff if you wanted to see their true character, and this move didn't bode well for her date.

"We're good," Terry said.

The server smiled again, but only to Sam, and left them.

Terry promptly took his fork and started digging into the meal. He looked up at her. "Your profile says you're widowed. Is that part true, at least?"

Sam nodded, bristling at the insinuation in his tone. She picked up her own fork and studied her dish to hide her annoyance. "Yes. Almost two years."

He nodded, continuing to chew. "I'm sorry to hear that. Were you married long?"

Sam shrugged, took a bite of her pasta. It was salty and sweet. Delicious. And she absolutely did not want to be here anymore, having this discussion. "About seven years."

Terry nodded again, grunted around a mouthful of food, and swallowed. "And so, what," he said, "you're ready to finally get back in the game again?"

Sam examined Terry as he shoveled another forkful of pasta in his mouth, his eyes on his plate.

She put her silverware down and risked an honest and vulnerable smile when he finally met her eyes.

"Truthfully," she said, "No. I'm not ready to get back in the game. I haven't quite figured out what I'm ready to do yet."

Terry stopped chewing, his face frozen above his plate. He stared at Sam, and she could feel the annoyance emanating from him. She closed her mouth.

Finally, Terry said, "Then why are you putting a dating profile out there? If you're not ready to start dating?"

Sam said nothing. She had no answer for him.

Terry swallowed and purposely placed his fork next to the dish. "That's just… *lying,* right? You say you want to go out on a date and then just pull this kind of bullshit?"

Sam's heart hammered in her chest. She was baffled at how the situation had taken such a turn. From the corner of her eyes, she could see the other diners reacting to Terry's volume. He was obviously struggling to control himself, but it was boiling over.

"Bullshit," Terry repeated. "This is fucking bullshit."

She could feel the warmth rising up her cheeks. "Terry," she said quietly, calmly. "I'm sorry. I didn't mean to lead you on. I thought this was just a date. You know, get to know each other."

"Obviously it's not 'just a date'," Terry seethed. "Because you had no intention of following through on it."

"What are you talking about?"

His eyes flashed. "Why are you making dating profiles when you have no intention of following through?"

Sam's shock turned to disbelief, then anger. "My friend made the profile for me," she hissed, "because she thought I needed to dip my toes back into society again. After my husband *fucking died,* you prick."

She stood up, opened her purse, and tossed a couple of twenties on the table. Swiftly slipping into her jacket she continued, "And against my better judgement, I did 'follow through' on it. You asked me out on a date, you little turd. Nothing more. And the date is over."

Terry stood up. "Well shit," he said, hands out. "Wait a second…"

She stopped and studied the man for a moment, sneering. "Oh, fuck off," she said, and stormed out of the restaurant.

Her hands were shaking the entire drive home as she replayed the conversation with Terry and wondered how it had turned so abruptly. What had she said that had set him off?

She was hurt and embarrassed, but also more than a little proud of herself that she had not burst into tears yet. It seemed she was finally all cried out.

When she pulled into her driveway, she considered heading right over to Kim's, then decided she would just text her after she washed off her makeup. Besides, Kim's place already looked dark.

While Sam flipped through her keys, her mind continued replaying the shitshow of her first date in many years, and she missed the late model Camry that slunk in and parked at the end of the block, swiftly turning off its headlights.

Sam locked the front door behind her, draping her jacket on the back of the couch. As she kicked off her shoes, she pulled out her phone and typed a quick text to her landlord:

You will not believe what happened tonight.
P.S. I HATE YOU

Thumbing the send button, she unbuttoned her pants and headed up the staircase.

Next door, Kim slept deeply on her couch, bathed in flickering television light and snoring heroically after ingesting a couple of her favorite gummies.

The television's volume was muted, but if Kim's own snoring couldn't wake her, then what chance did her phone have as it lit up brightly and buzzed on the coffee table?

Samantha's message had arrived but would go unread.

Sam turned off the tap water in the bathroom and paused scrubbing her face, listening carefully. Was that the doorbell?

A second later came a knocking from downstairs, and she patted her face dry and tied her bathrobe shut, shaking her head.

What did you expect? Kim to text you back like a normal human?

Down the slender staircase and into the living room she went, eager to share the evening's adventure, and as she threw open the front door she was already admonishing her landlord.

"Oh, you bitch," Sam said with a huge smile. "I can't believe I let you talk me into-"

Standing on the stoop outside was Terry, one eyebrow raised as she trailed off. He grinned at her, and her fury was instantaneous.

"No," she said, shaking her head. "No. No way."

He spread his hands out, smiling. "Wait," he said. "Please. I was a complete dick tonight, and I owe you a huge apology."

Sam fought to keep her face neutral. "Fine. Apology accepted, now please-"

He interrupted her with a wave, his smile brilliant. "Why don't we start this night over," he said, extending his hand for her to shake. "Hi. I'm Terry. I promise I'm not an asshole."

Sam ignored the hand, her mouth tightening. "Terry," she said, "You shouldn't be here. I appreciate what you're trying to do, but you showing up here is *not* cool. Did you fucking follow me?"

Without waiting for an answer, she closed the door. But Terry swiftly extended his foot, halting its movement.

He shook his head, the smile disappearing, astounded at her attitude. "Holy shit," he said. "I give you a chance to fix this monumental fuck-up, and you just keep digging the hole deeper and deeper."

Sam's eyes narrowed and she pushed against the door, trying to force it shut. Terry stood his ground, and she went ice-cold. "Terry," she said through gritted teeth, "You get the fuck off my property, or I swear I'm calling the cops *right now.*"

Terry's eyes flashed, suddenly scary-crazy. "Yeah?" he shouted, his volume rising. "Yeah?" He rammed his shoulder against the door, flinging it open and sending Sam to the floor.

He walked right into the house, grabbing the edge of the door and slamming it shut behind him. "Why don't you just go ahead and do that, you fucking whore?!?"

Sam, terrified and realizing now how serious the situation had become, scrambled to her feet and let out a bone-chilling scream at top volume, hoping someone – anyone - would hear.

෪

Both crows and ravens play significant roles in a number of different mythologies throughout history.

In Celtic legends, the phantom queen Morrighan would often manifest as a crow or have them by her side. She incited warriors to do battle and was seen as a guardian figure.

Native Americans often saw crows and ravens as tricksters, but some tribes believed the corvids were stealers of souls, or even responsible for giving sunlight to mankind.

The Norse believed them to be agents of Odin, his spies among the human world, and the Greeks saw them as a symbol of Apollo in his role as a god of prophecy.

Crows are exceptionally intelligent and have learned to adapt to the towns and cities that have encroached upon the natural world, building aeries on eaves and rooftops, even using anti-bird spikes to construct their nests.

They can recognize and differentiate between human faces and have a complex communication system that scientists still can't explain.

On the old wood fence surrounding Sam's backyard, six crows stood vigil, much later in the evening than they should normally be out, alert, on-guard.

In some mythologies, six crows together was a sign that death was nearby.

But these six crows seemed focused on the suited figure in the backyard's little garden, *Charlie's Garden*, to be precise, previously known as *Gwendolyn's Garden*.

That scarecrow had been built to keep the birds away from Blue Charlie, and the plan was clearly working. The rose bush had never looked healthier, his canes and tendrils swaying slowly like tiny, thorny snakes.

Blue wound through the entirety of the black suit and beyond now, a twisting, twisted mockery of musculature made of rose canes, branches, and thorns, filling the suit as a human body might, but also threatening to engulf it. Still, as intimidating as the figure was, it was immobile, inanimate.

But then…

The night air was pierced by Samantha's scream, and the scarecrow suddenly jolted to life, his head thrown back as if wracked in electrifying agony.

All six crows took to the air, startled. But they did not leave. They shrieked wildly, circling the scarecrow that was thrashing against his bonds and the twine that fastened him to the crossed garden poles.

His legs, unbound, snapped free from their roots in the dirt, tiny rose tendrils undulating against the ground, and he turned his expressionless mask to examine the garden post to which his arms were secured.

The crows were furious. This was an affront. This was not allowed. They cawed and attacked the scarecrow, diving and shrieking as the garden pole snapped at one elbow.

Sam scrambled from the living room and through the kitchen towards the back door. She threw the top bolt open, yanking on the door, but the doorknob remained immovable, still locked.

Quickly unlocking the knob, she yanked forcefully on the door, but it wouldn't budge. The top bolt was still locked.

What? I just-

Terry was coming for her, his eyes crazed, berserk. Sam side-stepped the man as he reached for her, spinning towards the front door again.

She dashed from the kitchen, caught off guard as an under-counter cabinet door suddenly flew open of its own accord, slamming against her hip and nearly sending her to the floor.

What the fuck? Did that just happen? Or did she just imagine it? *Oh, God. It's the ghost! That fucking ghost is REAL and it's attacking me*

She continued towards the front door, eyes wide with terror and disbelief, limping now, her hip sore and stinging.

"Run, you bitch!" Terry shouted behind her. "I like it when you run!"

The crows continued to dive bomb Blue Charlie, shrieking fiercely as he violently snapped the other end of the pole holding his arm.

The shattered bits of the garden post tumbled from his sleeves to the ground, and with both arms now free, Charlie reached up to the last of the twine wrapped around the bundle of canes that made up his throat.

Twiggy, thorned fingers ripped at the twine, finally snapping it, releasing him to the ground.

Straining against the rest of the bush he was still connected with, the scarecrow took a halting step towards the house, branches tearing and snapping until he stood apart, a thorny, wooden man in a black suit and stone mask.

A kamikaze crow dove too close, and Charlie's arm shot out, slapping the bird with one smashing blow to the ground. It lay silent and unmoving.

Blue Charlie's masked face turned towards the house.

Sam raced through the living room, eyes locked on the front door. She saw movement from the corner of her eye, the end of the couch springing at her as if tossed by a strongman.

It slammed into her leg hard enough to change her trajectory and send her sprawling to the floor in front of the narrow stairwell with a terrified shout.

No! Why now? Why is it attacking me now?

Terry stopped in front of her, oblivious to the supernatural happenings, intent on his prey. He grunted as he stared into her open bathrobe. "Goddammit," he leered. "Look at you. You are fun-sized, aren't you?"

Sam pulled herself up the first step of the staircase, crawling backwards now, just trying to put some space between her and this fucking lunatic. How had she misjudged him so completely?

Terry bent and grabbed her ankle. Sam, energized by terror, kicked out at him with her free leg. He got a hand on that ankle as well and dragged her back down the stairs, her head thudding painfully against each wooden step.

She found her voice and screamed again, terror and horror and pain wrapped in fear, the volume loud enough to shred her throat.

Terry responded by grasping a handful of her hair, dragging her to her feet and delivering a brutal punch to her face, a single blow on the side of her chin that nearly rendered her unconscious.

"Keep screaming, you cunt," he spat, "and I'll fucking kill you. You got that? *I'll fuck you and I'll kill you.*"

She nodded, dazed, tears streaming down her face. Her eyes wouldn't focus, and that terrified her.

Terry grinned, her hair still gripped in his fist, and he pushed aside the hem of her robe, exposing a breast and nipple.

He met her eyes, enjoying her tears. "Great tits," he said, but she wasn't looking at him, now. Her eyes were full of terror, surprise, even shock… but they were locked over his shoulder, and he released her quickly, suddenly realizing there was a presence behind him.

He whirled, primed to fight her landlord or a neighbor, but he was utterly unprepared for what stood behind him.

It was a man in a dirty black suit, and Terry thought briefly that he must be homeless – the man's hands and feet were filthy and looked to be covered in dirt and sticks.

Stranger still was the mask the man wore, a featureless face with black holes for eyes and an annoying smirk on its lips.

Terry sneered, trying to hide how unnerving the visage was. "The fuck are you supposed to be?"

He aimed a quick blow at the man's face, striking the mask and dislodging it, sending it clattering to the floor.

But underneath the mask was madness. Twisted rose branches that formed cheeks, lips, eyebrows… a wooden mockery of a human face. The eyes, moving impossibly in their sockets, rigid and textured and *fibrous*, following Terry unerringly.

He recoiled in horror, taking two steps back, and Blue Charlie seethed with fury, his wooden eyebrows furrowed in a menacing, impossible expression.

The wooden man reached out like lightning, savagely slapping at Terry's face with one ferocious blow.

Terry staggered backwards, the lower half of his face scored with deep, bloody fissures that exposed muscle and even bone in some places. Ribbons of skin hung from his chin as blood suddenly poured down his neck and chest, sopping his shirt.

Charlie took a moment to examine his wooden and thorny hands, as if surprised at the damage they were capable of.

Sam, sprawled at the base of the stairwell, stared with shocked and horrified eyes at the sight of the living scarecrow and the destruction caused to Terry's once-handsome face.

Her attention was dragged back to the thing in the dirty black suit, a suit that was very familiar to her. The creature was made of wood, twigs and branches that almost seemed to *writhe* as he moved, as if they were growing, growing unnaturally fast, like… like…

"No," she said, "no, no, no…"

Terry brought trembling hands to the ruins of his face, too afraid to actually touch it. His shredded skin hung from his skull, his eyes wide and glassy, and he stumbled towards the door, trying to skirt around and escape the suited monster.

But Blue Charlie would have none of it. As Terry staggered past, Charlie slapped at him again, this time striking the man's throat, shredding the flesh and the muscle underneath, slicing open the artery, blood spurting wildly as Terry was sent spinning and gurgling to the floor, his mouth twitching as the life left him.

He hit the floor hard, a blow that would have knocked him out, eyes still open but already losing their shine. His blood, thick and dark, pumped and pooled around his face.

Charlie stared emotionlessly at the dead man, his wooden eyes unreadable. From behind him came a single, cracked, terrified sob, and he turned his head with an audible creak towards Samantha.

She shrank under the wooden man's strange gaze, his face crawling with impossible movement. She could taste blood in her mouth. She thought Terry might have loosened a tooth. "Get away from me," she whispered.

In the scarecrow's shadow, Terry's lifeless eyes stared at Sam from where he lay in his own cooling blood, accusing her of the state he was in. Dead, ravaged, mangled on her living room floor.

But then the dead man's eyelid suddenly twitched, and Sam gasped, bringing a hand to her bloody mouth. His eyes rolled unnaturally in their sockets, and his shoulders jerked with life.

Placing his palms flat against the floor, Terry pushed, raising himself up, his bloody face squelching as it pulled from the already sticky pool it had been resting in on the hardwood floor.

And then Terry got to his feet. He was quite clearly dead, and yet he stood, swaying back and forth, his face and throat a bloody, meaty mess, as he confronted his victim and his killer.

Sam moaned, a sound that bordered on lunacy, on madness, her mind threatening to crack wide open, her eyes wide with horror and revulsion and monumental disbelief of the two creatures in her living room.

Blue Charlie turned to face Terry, who put his hands out in an almost comical, "hear me out"-kind of motion. A maddening giggle danced on Sam's lips at the sight of the dead man, but she tamped it down. If she started laughing now, she was sure she'd never be able to stop.

And then Terry smiled. Not the evil, lecherous grin Sam had seen as he looked at her exposed body, but a warm, genuine smile, as if greeting a long-lost friend.

"Glaggly," he gurgled happily to the wooden monster in front of him. His face was a dripping, mangled mockery of teeth and tongue, but he seemed to recognize the wooden man.

In response, Blue Charlie lunged towards the living corpse, placing his thorny hands on either side of Terry's head. In one savage motion, he twisted with such force that the man's head was torn completely from his body. The headless corpse stood for a moment before toppling to the side.

Sam screamed again, and Charlie turned to face her, dropping Terry's head to the floor. He took two steps towards her, and her mind finally surrendered to the onslaught, her eyes rolling to the whites, her head slumping to the floor.

Charlie stood above her, staring down at her soft, bare skin, and then at the headless body leaking all over the floor next to her.

After a few moments of consideration, he stooped, grabbed Terry's decapitated corpse by one leg, and dragged him through the kitchen and out the back door.

Outside, several crows immediately set upon Blue Charlie, diving and attacking. He ignored them, dragging Terry's body to the tiny garden in the darkness.

∞∞

Sam stirred, sensing the warmth of the sun filtering through the bedroom windows. She turned her head towards the light, and the sudden lance of pain in her jaw brought all of last night's memories crashing down upon her.

That fucker Terry had attacked her. In her own home. And something else had been there, too. Some kind of... creature. There was no other word for the monstrous wooden man.

What the fuck was *that thing?*

She reached up, delicately feeling at her face, wincing at the contact. Taking a quick mental inventory, she noted she was still in her robe and someone had put her in her bed.

When Sam stood, a mild wave of dizziness swept over her. She waited for it to pass, then moved slowly and quietly towards the stairwell.

As she reached the first floor, the silence of the house struck her. The emptiness was palpable.

There was a large pool of tacky blood at the base of the stairwell, and the scarecrow's theatrical mask lay upside down on the floor. The memory of Terry's head being twisted off in her scarecrow protector's hands sprang up, and she fought back the blackness that crept in on the edge of her vision.

From that pool of blood ran a crimson streak the length of the living room to the kitchen, but Terry's body was nowhere to be seen.

Sam stepped over the bloody smear and stood next to the front door. She paused with her hand on the doorknob, freedom and safety calling from only two steps away.

Jesus, run NOW. You're home free.

But she let go of the handle and turned back towards the bloody trail, following it stealthily into the kitchen. The thick smear continued across the linoleum and disappeared out the open back door.

Sam slunk to the sink, almost crouching as she walked, in an effort to stay unseen from outside.

Peeking over the windowsill of the cracked window, she saw the scarecrow standing calmly in his filthy black suit at the edge of the garden, the dirt of which had been torn apart and disturbed and then covered again. She could see tendrils of the rosebush already sprouting in that dirt.

At the recently animated scarecrow's feet lay two dead crows and multiple broken rose branches and canes.

He tore himself from the garden. To come help me.

Sam couldn't see his face, but he seemed to be studying the tiny, leaning sign that read *Charlie's Garden.*

A golden sunbeam pierced through the clouds, and after a moment, the scarecrow stretched his hand delicately towards the light.

I need my camera, she thought, but did not move.

As his furrowed, wooden fingers entered the sunbeam, a green bud erupted on the back of his hand, swiftly flowering into a beautiful celeste blue rose, and then quickly wilting into a blackish-purple nub that detached from his body, falling to the ground.

Sam gasped, bringing a hand up to her mouth in wonder. She stood at the sink for several minutes, watching as the rosebush-man soaked up the sunlight that inched across his body.

Finally, she stepped out onto the patio as silently as possible, her eyes never leaving the spectacle.

Two crows sat on the back fence, squawking but not moving, kept at bay by the bodies of their dead brothers near the scarecrow's feet.

As Sam watched, another rose bud appeared on the back of the creature's hand, blooming over the course of several seconds, and then withering quickly, a complete life cycle in less than a minute.

She approached in awe. Another bud burst into beautiful, sky-blue petals on the back of his head, and just as swiftly began to die. She reached towards him, unable to stop herself.

The scarecrow spun, aware of her now, startling her out of her fascination, and the two of them stood that way, regarding each other - her in her bathrobe with a bruised chin and dried blood on her lip, and him a woody, thorny man in a dirty, bloody, black suit.

"What *are* you," Sam whispered, dropping her hand.

The scarecrow worked his mouth, but no sound emerged. Sam was entranced by the movement and emotions on his face. He seemed confused, at a loss to answer her question, even if he'd been able to speak.

Instead, he turned towards the torn-up garden, the broken garden posts, and then motioned to the tilted sign that read *Charlie's Garden*. He turned back to Samantha, and she could see the bewilderment in his strange eyes.

A million emotions washed over her at once - disbelief, fear, wonder, awe - all cycling through her as quickly as the blooming of the rosebuds on the creature's wooden musculature.

"…Charlie?" she asked, feeling immediately foolish. "No. This isn't real. You can't be real. You *died.*"

Blue Charlie opened his mouth, as confused as she was, but no sound emerged. Frightened and disoriented, he reached out to her, and as he did, a single, gorgeous blue rose bloomed from his palm.

It mirrored the author photo of Charlie's book, the photo Sam had loved and taken herself, and she burst into tears and rushed to him, wrapping her arms around him and pressing her face against his hard, unyielding chest.

"Oh, God," she nearly sobbed. "Charlie! It *is* you! Somehow, I knew that everything happening with Blue was *you*… watching me… looking out for me."

Surprised at first, Blue Charlie enfolded her in his arms and she grabbed his head in both hands, sobbing and standing on tiptoes to pepper his wood face with kisses.

Sam's desperation awakened something within him, and he suddenly clutched her body, embracing her firmly.

She met his wooden eyes, grotesque but somehow beautiful, rigid and yet full of movement, moisture, *life*. He stared back at her and they were both engulfed in the moment. The insanity of the entire situation, the danger, the horror, the sheer impossibility… it erupted into senseless passion.

Kissing him intensely, she tasted the earth, the green, the primal life of the planet, and he responded in kind, his tongue sharp and unyielding.

Sam closed the drapes on the bedroom window, muting the tone of the room to a dim orange that faintly illuminated the two figures standing near the bed.

She shrugged Blue Charlie's jacket from his shoulders, tossing it aside, and as she kissed him again, her fingers found the buttons on his white shirt, unfastening them. The short, sharp thorns of his biceps caught and snagged on the shirt as she slid it from his body.

Her bathrobe fell to the floor, and she watched his strange, wooden eyes take in her body. Charlie had made no secret in the past of how much he'd loved every inch of Sam's skin, and it seemed nothing had changed.

She tilted her head to kiss him again, and her flesh caught on a thorn. She flinched and hissed at the pain.

Blue Charlie jerked away from her at the sound, but Sam was insistent. It was a genuine, sensual moment - brief pain surrounded by bliss and irrepressible craving, and so it was allowed.

She grabbed Charlie by the elbow, pulling him back to her and pressing her soft, fragile flesh against his hard, painful skin with an intensity that underscored the harsh reality of the situation: if they chose to proceed, it was going to hurt.

And it *did* hurt, when he entered her, God it hurt, stinging and tearing at her insides. But it didn't hurt as much as the last eighteen months without The Love of Her Life had, no, it didn't hurt like that, and so she endured it, she *welcomed* it, wrapping her legs tighter around him, the tears flowing freely as she whispered how much she missed him into his prickly ear, and when he put his sharp, wooden fingers around her throat, she moaned in both pain and pleasure.

Afterwards, they lay next to each other in the bed, the sweat cooling on Sam's flesh, stinging the hundreds of tiny cuts and welts that crisscrossed and covered her.

The sheets were full of snags and tears, dotted with bloody drops and smears. Sam smiled, euphoric despite the pain. Sometimes wishes came true.

Blue Charlie stared at the ceiling, his bizarre eyes darting back and forth, his memories jumbled, confused.

A noise came to him, and he glanced toward the open bedroom door, to the hallway beyond. To the bathroom down the hallway. An echoing sound from that deep bathtub, from that black hole of a drain…

It was the sound of a young girl sobbing.

4

Kim woke to early light streaming across her face. She stretched and felt the crick her neck would be complaining about all day from sleeping on the couch.

The television was still on, but silent. She reached for the remote to turn it off and her eye caught the blinking LED at the top of her cell phone. Sitting up stiffly, she thumbed the phone on and saw a notification from Sam had come in at some time during the night. But more important, Kim's niece, Lauren, had texted four messages and a voicemail, and that set off klaxons in Kim's mind.

Lauren was the daughter of Kim's older sister, Colleen, who had passed a few years back from liver failure. Lauren was smart and resourceful, and lived in Sunset with her long time fiancé, the last time Kim had checked. If the girl was reaching out to Kim for help, something dire had happened, and the girl had no one else to turn to.

Lauren's voicemail related in strained and stressed tones that her fiancé had been killed in a work accident overnight, and Lauren hoped Kim could come pick up her great-niece, Katie, in Sunset, and deliver her to her grandfather in Kobbe's End today.

Kim wasn't a huge fan of children (even those related to her), and she hadn't seen Lauren since her mom's funeral a few years back, but the girl was clearly at her wit's end. A trip from Heather to Sunset, and then to Kobbe's End and back to Heather promised to be a six hour affair, and the crick in Kim's neck groaned loudly at the thought. But what choice did she have? Family trumped all else.

She called her niece and told her how sorry she was to hear about her fiancé (*Adam*, Kim thought his name was), and that she would absolutely help in any way the girl needed.

Throwing on some mismatched clothing, Kim left her house without checking her hair or makeup. As she pulled out of her driveway, she texted Samantha:

Emergency situation has popped up, should be back this evening.

Her finger hovered over the send button for a moment, then she added:

Sounds like we both have stories to share.

And she pulled out of the driveway and aimed her old Isuzu in the direction the dawn had recently cracked from.

If Heather was the crown-jewel of The Treble, then the town of Sunset, WA, was surely the armpit of Kobbe County, a dusty, unpleasant town that consisted of a long Main Street with a few sad cafés and restaurants, and several cross streets that branched out to the small church, or the school, or the Post Office.

The town's only claim to fame seemed to be the local junkyard, a rat-infested maze of stacked, crushed cars that was as big as a small town itself.

Driving into town, Kim noted the gigantic construction site covered in signage that proclaimed it as the future location of Sunset Gas, a truck stop/restaurant/grocery store that promised to bring dozens of jobs to the town while simultaneously putting out of business Hezel's Auto Shop, the tiny, two car garage and gas station on the corner tucked behind the huge construction.

Kim drove past the bustling workers and machinery, wondering morbidly which one of the big rigs had taken the life of her niece's fiancé, the father of Kim's own great-niece.

When Kim pulled up to Lauren's house, the girl was barely holding it together. She was a wreck, her eyes red and cried out, and obviously very grateful for Kim's help.

Her daughter, Katie, only five years old, wasn't aware of the details, but she was smart enough to suss out that something was going on, especially when her estranged aunt suddenly showed up.

"I really appreciate this," Lauren said. "Like, *really.* I know you and my dad don't get along very well."

That was an understatement. Lauren's dad was something just shy of a complete asshole, and Kim had been dead set against her sister marrying the man many years ago. But against all odds they'd stayed married, and then had Lauren, who had turned out to be a pretty dang wonderful human being.

Kim sighed. "None of that matters right now. I'm happy to help in any way I can."

So then Lauren showed Kim how to lock in Katie's car seat in the back of her ancient Isuzu. She strapped her daughter in with practiced ease. "You be good on the drive with Aunty Kim," she said. "I'll meet you at Pee-Paw's tonight."

The little girl smiled and gave her mom a comical thumbs up. "Roger," she said, and Kim chuckled, envying the resilience of the young.

The drive to Kobbe's End included several games of counting the colors of the cars on the road, a couple spirited rounds of "The Song that Never Ends", and a story by Katie recounting her dad pretending to be an enraged ape, leaping and grunting and beating on the furniture in the living room. Kim smiled at the story, but the thought of the little girl never getting another chance to see her father goofing off like that made the older woman deeply sad, and she was grateful that Katie fell asleep shortly thereafter.

A little over an hour later, Kim took the first exit into Kobbe's End, driving past the boarded-up windows of shops and restaurants that didn't survive the COVID closures. She hadn't visited the 'End in years and sighed heavily when she saw the homeless encampment of tents and lean-tos filling a vacant lot.

From the back seat, Katie said, "Why are all those people camping there?"

Kim's eyes found the little girls' in the rear-view mirror. "I guess they're on vacation," she said, and then quietly, "and also, the world is falling apart."

"Daddy says the world is completely fucked," Katie said, her eyes thoughtful as they passed boarded up businesses and a small, old church with a dead lawn.

And only getting more fucked up every day, Kim wanted to say. Instead, she responded with, "That's a bad word. Don't say that."

She skirted the lake on the far end of town and pulled into Abel Helman's driveway only a few minutes later.

Her widowed brother-in-law sauntered outside to greet them, frosty at first - they hadn't seen each other since Colleen's funeral - but he invited her in for a soda and a bathroom break if she needed one.

Kim gratefully accepted the offer of a bathroom that wasn't one of the two sketchy rest areas between Heather and Kobbe's End.

While relieving herself, she texted Samantha again, asking if she was all right. She was a little worried that her renter hadn't responded yet.

When she came back out, Katie was already in the back yard, playing on the swing set her grandparents had built for her years ago, and Abel had poured them both a glass of Coca-Cola.

"Can I put a little Jack in that?" Abel asked her.

"Hell yes," Kim replied, surprised at the offer.

And the two of them watched Katie play while they consumed two Jack and Cokes each, and discussed how difficult it was to lose someone you loved, how relationships are like addictions, and going through withdrawals are a real motherfucking bitch. And when Kim left, Abel embraced her and told her to take care of herself, and she thought maybe they had achieved something positive today amidst all this tragedy.

Kim sent Samantha another text as she left Kobbe's End that afternoon, and then another when she ended up stopping at one of those sketchy rest areas anyway, on her way back to Heather.

She was getting a bit worried at the silence on Samantha's end, and had decided when she finally got home, her first stop would be at the house next door.

But only a few minutes later, a text from Samantha arrived that read:

Sorry, I am very sick right now. We'll talk soon. Lots to tell you about when I feel better. Please don't come over, I'm staying in bed and don't want to get you sick.

Kim exhaled, relieved. As much as she wanted to hear about Samantha's date, it had been an exceedingly long day, and she was exhausted. Home and gummy-infused sleep sounded delightful.

∞CB

The sun had moved to the other side of the house, and Sam's bedroom was bathed in deep blue when she woke up again.

Her phone vibrated from the nightstand, and she groggily slapped in its direction.

Pain struck from all directions, tiny, stinging cuts covering her skin, and deeper, sharper agony from inside her, and she gasped and groaned as her hand found the phone.

Gritting her teeth, she twisted into a less painful position and brought the phone to her face, scrolling through multiple messages from her landlord:

Are you all right?
Call me.
I'm starting to get worried.
CALL ME
WHAT'S GOING ON

Sam groaned. *Fuck. How am I supposed to explain this?*

She was still processing everything that had happened in the last twenty-four hours herself, and definitely wasn't prepared to explain that her dead husband's soul was somehow residing in the human-shaped rose bush that was named after him.

After a moment's consideration, Sam texted a reply to Kim:

Sorry, I am very sick right now. We'll talk soon. Lots to tell you about when I feel better. Please don't come over, I'm staying in bed and don't want to get you sick.

Thumbing the send button, she dropped the phone on the torn and blood-spotted sheets next to her. She winced, covering it with a smile, and turned to Charlie's side of the bed.

But it was empty.

Blue Charlie's thorny fingers snagged on the weave of the old couch as he surveyed the living room, his eyes roaming from corner to corner, his mind jumbled, frenetic. Reeling.

What had happened to him? This body, this mass of sinewy, living branches was a horror show, an impossibility, but he could not remember what had come before it. He'd been... *alive*, once. And then... *not*. He could recall that, even if everything else felt like smoke slipping through his fingers.

The memories were splintered, like the root ball he'd torn himself from outside, fractured images without context and meaning, his only linear memories starting when he'd awakened to find himself crucified in the garden.

Charlie's Garden.

But he was inside, now. Was this his house? Was this even his couch? Some of these things felt familiar, a flash of recall, a whisper of a memory that quickly faded... but others were utterly foreign.

He lowered himself into the easy chair, continuing to take stock of the space. The dimly lit room held a palpable energy, something he could almost feel, almost remember...

And then it was gone again.

Snatching up the book on the side table, he turned it over in his hands. On the back was a photo of a rugged man holding a blue rose. The same as the roses that blossomed uncontrollably from his own wooden skin.

He recognized the flower in the photo, but not the man.

The book was titled *No Rose Without the Thorn*, and opening it to the dedication page revealed a short inscription:

> *as always,*
> *for babydoll*

Blue Charlie's lips parted as if to speak, but no sound emerged. He tried again, managing only a slight rasp. He could feel his body changing, moving, *creating*. His throat stretched and tingled where green, prickly tendrils were slowly creating new muscle, tissue... vocal cords. He wondered if the buzzing in his ears was the green brain inside his wooden head, strange synapses moving, growing, and then firing off, hopefully bringing back his memories.

A dozen books tumbled from the bookshelf along the wall, thumping loudly and scattering to the floor.

Startled, Charlie stood, the thorns on his legs snagging and tearing at his dirty black slacks.

The room was empty, but there was a presence here with him. The books could not have fallen by themselves. He stooped to retrieve them, eyes wary.

Sam, dressed in her bathrobe again, peeked around the corner of the stairwell. She watched the wooden man with a mixture of awe and fear, but when he looked up and caught her staring, she smiled.

Standing, Charlie attempted to return the smile and placed the books back on the shelf they had fallen from.

"Charlie," Sam murmured. "Hi. I have to admit, I thought maybe none of this was real."

His wooden eyes drifted from her face as she bared a savagely scratched arm.

"Although," she continued, "There is certainly plenty of evidence."

She lingered there awkwardly, watching him think. He was clearly overwhelmed with everything that was happening.

So am I, she thought. *I just had sex with a fucking rosebush.*

Her eyes caught the bloody smear across the hardwood floor and a wave of nausea washed over her.

Fucking Terry. Where is he?

Somewhere out back, she hoped. It was going to take some elbow grease to clean up all of this blood.

Sam marveled at her composure, already thinking about the mop and bucket in the kitchen pantry.

Her stomach rumbled suddenly. "Are you hungry?" she asked. "I'm starving."

She paused as a thought occurred to her. "I mean… do you eat?"

Blue Charlie opened his mouth, but all that came out was a breathy rasp. He pursed his wooden lips and shrugged, as if to say *this is all new to me, too.*

Sam wrung out the bloody mop and watched as Charlie voraciously shoveled another burger patty between his wooden lips.

Where does it go, she wondered. *The branches had reformed themselves into musculature to mimic human form. Had they done the same with internal organs? Did he have a rose cane stomach? A thorny heart? A head full of wooden brains? Was he breathing? And if so… how?*

Was there a soul inside all of that wood? A magical void trapped by the rosebush, somehow?

Photos. We need to document this.

Charlie devoured the last of the hamburgers whole, and Sam shook her head in wonder. "Wow…"

She'd thrown six burgers on the electric grill and while they cooked, she started mopping up the dried blood that was smeared throughout the kitchen and living room. She didn't think it would pass a CSI investigation, but it didn't look like a murder scene anymore.

His cut-stem eyes met hers and he smiled as he chewed.

Sam smiled back, gently squeezing his shoulder. She could feel the thorns poking through his shirt. "I know," she said. "I know. It's been two years. You must be starving."

Charlie looked up at her again, his eyes unfathomable. Nodding thoughtfully, he reached for the stemless wine glass she'd filled for him and took a large gulp to wash everything down, then made a face, pushing the glass away.

"Wow," Sam said, "That's your favorite Malbec from Walla Walla!"

Charlie shook his head in distaste.

Sam filled a glass of water and handed it to him. He drank it gratefully. She took a sip from the glass of wine. Delicious. Had she expected a green, living thing to survive on anything but water? For whatever passed for tastebuds on his wooden tongue to appreciate the complexities of wine immediately? It did seem a lot to ask.

She went back to the sink, continuing to wring the bloody mop and rinsing it all down the drain. Her eyes drifted to the garden outside, and the remains of the rosebush Charlie had torn himself from. It continued to grow from its broken stumps, its thorny canes and tendrils snaking out of the garden and stacking up against the house's foundation now, as if trying to rejoin Charlie.

The garden itself was a mess of torn up dirt and mud, and Charlie's sign tilted like a gravestone marker from an old black-and-white horror flick.

The crows were back on the fence, squawking as they jockeyed for space around each other, keeping an eye on everything, but apparently uninterested in attacking the rosebush anymore.

She turned off the tap, noting the blood smeared on the patio outside. "What did you… *do*… with Terry?"

Without looking back at Charlie, she felt him get up and move to stand behind her, his hard, unforgiving hands on her shoulders. Sam stiffened under their prickly pressure, but slowly relaxed.

Blue Charlie removed one hand and motioned towards the garden outside.

Sam looked at the fresh mud and dirt of the garden and understood immediately. "Oh, God," she said, then looked over her shoulder at him. "I mean, good. He would have…" she shuddered. "I need you to know, I didn't do anything with him. Or *anyone*. It was just a stupid idea to get me out of the house finally after you had…" she trailed off. "I'm so sorry."

His hands ran down her arms and dug into her hips as he kissed her neck.

She winced. "What I really mean is 'thank you.' Thank you for coming back to me. Thank you for being here… when I needed you."

He undid the terry-cloth belt at her waist and slid the robe off her shoulders to the floor, his hands scraping painfully up her naked flesh, and as he cupped her breasts she leaned back against him.

He slid a hand up to her neck and she gasped in pain and not a little fear.

But it was not completely unwelcome, and they began moving together, both of them facing the window and the garden graveyard as he wrapped a thorny fist in her hair.

The crows screeched again, agitated now, angry as their lovemaking progressed, perhaps aware that the physical act was nearly unbearable for Sam.

But love is not just physical, and she closed her eyes and bit the fat part of her palm and moaned through the pain. Nothing she was going through now was any worse than what the last two years had forced upon her, and she'd already bargained her soul away multiple times to endure any and every suffering if it only meant she could have back the love of her life.

And here he was.

They saw everything, the crows, and they were not pleased. The blasphemous sex in the kitchen window, the decimated rosebush that continued to grow and spread like wildfire, the upset dirt and mud that covered Terry's decapitated corpse, among other things. This cursed parcel of land continued to rack up karmic debt that could never be paid, a stain upon the soil that would never wash clean, and the black birds continued their grumbling even after Sam and Charlie had taken their passion upstairs and out of sight.

ഇ○ഇ

Charlie's eyes were closed, but Sam couldn't tell if he was sleeping. Did he even need to sleep? His chest wasn't moving, but she didn't know if he breathed. If he even had lungs. She pushed away dark thoughts of the last time she'd seen him not breathing. The roses on his body were not blooming right now, and she thought that must mean something.

Do you dream? Can you dream? Are there synapses firing right now somehow through a brain made of thorny bark?

Or was she dreaming all of this herself? Had everything she'd experienced in the last two days happened in the blink of an eye in that moment just after Terry had clocked her on the chin? Would she come out of this dream at any second to find Terry choking her? Choking her... or worse?

No. She didn't believe that. The agony enveloping her body was too real. Too painful.

Their lovemaking had been more aggressive this last time, with Charlie taking control, a little rougher with her than she was prepared for.

She'd never been a prude, and Charlie had unleashed something in her during their relationship. A willingness to experiment, to cut loose. He'd brought a lighthearted kinkiness to their sex life that she'd enthusiastically embraced.

But this was not that. The way he'd held her down tonight had been... forceful. *Hurtful.* And not just because he was covered in tiny, sharp barbs.

He'd seemed to get more and more excited as her moans became increasingly painful. That wasn't like him.

Or was it?

Had she forgotten what their life had actually been like? Was there a little more strife in their relationship than she wanted to remember?

No. He'd been dead for almost two years, for chrissakes. And then been reborn into a body made of wood and roses. He was confused, traumatized. Who wouldn't be? This would take time to get used to. For both of them.

His bare chest was rough and bristly, a web of rose canes forming his skin and musculature. As she lightly traced a finger along them, it seemed for a moment she could feel the rhythm of a wooden heart beating deep within him. But then she snatched her hand away, startled, as she noticed his skin shifting - *growing*, almost imperceptibly, before her eyes. In the quiet that followed, she watched the canes press closer and closer together, as though striving to merge into a seamless expanse of smooth, unbroken wooden flesh.

It was the most beautiful thing she'd ever seen.

She crept out of the bloodstained bed, watching to see if he woke. When he didn't, she put on her robe and left the bedroom, closing the door noiselessly behind her.

Plugging the drain of the scratched and faded pink bathtub, she cranked the faucet all the way to 'HOT'.

As the water crashed into the tub, Sam lit the tea lights she'd placed around the bathroom, part of Kim's housewarming gift basket.

Steam fogged the mirror and filled the room, but the thought of turning the cold tap on never entered her mind.

When the tub was close to full, she turned the faucet off and set one foot in the steaming water. She gasped in pain and stepped in with the other foot, waiting for her skin to adjust to the heat.

Easing herself into the water brought tears to her eyes, each razor thin scratch and welt screaming in protest as she submerged them in the hot water.

Finally seating herself in the tub, the water between her legs bloomed pink and she groaned, her vision going dark around the edges.

She soaked in her agony for a moment, the steam rising as she bit her lip, fighting to control the pain.

Closing her eyes, she exhaled and submerged herself completely under the scalding pink water.

PART THREE

ROSE HIPS

NO ROSE WITHOUT THE THORN

"We'd climbed past the 12,000-foot mark when we hit a rockslide that had wiped out the rest of the trail. The path was buried beneath a mess of jagged stones, and for a moment, I thought we might be stuck. But after carefully picking our way through, we finally emerged on the other side, and that's when I saw it.

A tree of blue, stretching to the sky, climbing as high as a three-story building. The color was so vivid, so unexpected, that it stopped me in my tracks. It looked like nothing I'd ever seen—like a piece of the heavens had broken off and taken root right in front of us. And Sam—she was always the one to keep her cool—actually gasped. I swear I heard her whisper, "Oh, my God."

I couldn't help but smile, remembering Grandpa Howard's story. His blue rose, the one the locals had feared and cursed, had seemed like a myth. But standing there under that wild, blue bush, I knew without a doubt—his story had been true."

- Charles Perry
No Rose Without the Thorn

1

Something is definitely wrong.

Kim knew it. In the two days since she'd returned from Kobbe's End, she'd had zero contact with Samantha. Not for lack of trying. Kim had sent well over a dozen messages to her renter, but not one of them had received a response. She understood Samantha was sick, but so sick she couldn't text back even once?

Kim was also worried Samantha might be *very* sick. She could be dead, even, and wouldn't that be a lovely situation to deal with? She had a friend who died in his apartment a few years back during a heatwave, and the mess left by his liquifying body had not been easily cleaned up. A landlord's nightmare.

Much of her time in the last couple days had been spent making sure Lauren and little Katie were settling in well in Kobbe's End.

Yesterday, Lauren had asked her aunt if she'd be interested in accompanying them on a quick trip back to Sunset to pick up a few personal items, which Kim had agreed to. They caught up on the events of the last few years during lunch at the little Main Street Café in Sunset, discussing Adam's accident in carefully worded code to keep Katie in the dark.

Afterwards, Kim had picked up a little gift basket at the Witch House Apothecary and filled it with sage and selenite, abalone, and healing crystals. A full smudging kit that she padded out with plenty of incense and a little burner.

She grabbed it now as she left her house, heading across the lawn to her rental property next door.

The first thing she noticed were the crows. Dozens of the black birds crowded the eaves of the house and the short picket fence enclosing the front yard, all of them jostling for space while keeping a close eye on Kim as she approached the door.

She rang the doorbell once, then again as the crows began cawing, vigorously bobbing their heads as they squawked at her.

"Samantha," Kim called out, pounding on the door. "Samantha, open up. You're worrying me!"

She rang the doorbell again, hearing it chime inside the house and ready to use her spare key to discover exactly what she was dealing with inside. "If you don't answer the door, I'm coming -"

The doorknob clicked and twisted, the door opening just a hair.

"- in..." Kim trailed off.

Samantha peeked out and Kim stifled a gasp. Her renter's hair was a heroic mess, and the bags under her eyes were dark and puffy. She was in her robe and looked like she hadn't slept in days.

Keeping the door open only a crack, Samantha smiled weakly. "Kim," she said. "Hey."

"Oh my God. Are you okay? I haven't heard from you in days."

"Yeah. I'm very sick. Flu, I guess."

Kim winced. "Ugh," she said. "I am so sorry. I was worried about you! How can I help? Soup? Theraflu?"

"No," Samantha said quickly. "No, but thank you. I just need some rest."

"I can do some shopping for you if you want to put a list together."

"No. Please. I appreciate it, but I'm fine for food and Theraflu. I'd just like to be alone. Okay?"

"Of course," Kim said. "Please call if you need anything."

"I will. Thank you."

"I brought you a -"

Samantha closed the door and Kim hesitated for a moment, clutching the basket full of selenite and incense. She considered knocking again and just thrusting the basket into Samantha's hands if she answered, then thought better of it. Her renter had made it clear she wanted to be left alone.

Still gripping the basket's handle, Kim left the stoop. The crows eyed her suspiciously, giving no ground.

Sam closed the door and paused, turning her head towards the staircase, listening for any movement upstairs. After a reassuring moment of silence, she released the breath she had been carefully holding.

She limped towards the kitchen, each step an excruciating, grinding, lightning bolt of pain through her abdomen. She'd had to beg Charlie's forgiveness this morning, but her body needed a chance to heal if this were going to continue.

The activity of the specter inhabiting the home - Eldred Huxley, she now knew - had increased with the sexual relations between her and Charlie, as if the ghost were offended by anyone expressing love in the form of physical affection in this house.

At least it's not incest, you fucking creep.

She navigated her way through the maze of clutter that the living room had become, the floor covered with the books she had so carefully placed in the bookshelves, the area rugs flipped or askew, the furniture at odd angles, all due to Eldred Huxley's various tantrums over the last few days.

Sam had watched books and knickknacks fly off the shelves, propelled by a ghostly force, and often aimed directly at her. It terrified her each time.

But the ghost rarely dared to attack Charlie. Huxley's intense hatred seemed focused solely on Sam.

Whenever this happened, her wooden guardian would calm her, striding angrily through the room until the ghostly activity ceased. He seemed far less unnerved by the ghost than she was, and Sam conceded he had more on his mind than she right now. His very existence continued to befuddle the rosebush man.

Charlie attempted to speak regularly now, but could still only muster a guttural rasping sound, much to his great frustration.

Sam was confident it would come. His body continued to grow, to thicken, to solidify. Already, his wooden form had grown together so densely that there were no longer any gaps or major seams between the rose canes that formed his wiry frame.

If only he weren't so… sharp, she thought, wincing at the wave of pain that nearly staggered her again.

He could be a little gentler, a smaller, quieter voice in her head said, and she swiftly tamped it down.

Sunlight streamed through the cracked window as she eased herself into the chair at the kitchen table. Her laptop was open and still on the city records page she'd been surfing when Kim knocked.

Taking a sip from her coffee, she squirmed and groaned, attempting to find a position that didn't agonize her.

Her eyes were drawn to the small, square heater vent at the kitchen's baseboard, and the several thin, thorny vines that protruded from the old metal grate. The rosebush outside had recovered and grown to impossible proportions, but instead of getting taller it had crept along the concrete patio towards the back door, and then up along the foundation, slipping underneath the old wood siding of the house like nothing she'd ever seen before.

Sam wondered how deep into the house Blue Charlie had invaded. She could see the extruded outline of vines under the wallpaper along the kitchen walls and thought the rose bush might have reached the living room already.

The narrow spaces between the walls and studs must have been a crowded and crisscrossed mess of buds and thorns like the vacant lot full of blackberries next door.

But why?

The bush outside seemed determined to rejoin its human-shaped nucleus, which now resided within the house.

Sam didn't want to think about how Kim would react to the thorny vegetation that was spreading through her rental property from the outside in, at what could only be described as an alarming rate.

She didn't enjoy lying to her new friend, but what other options did she have? Try to explain the magic that had happened here? Attempt to impress upon Kim that True Love's return trumped everything? Charlie had somehow found his way back to the land of the living, and there was nothing Sam would allow to come between them again.

Still, there was one troublesome fly in this ointment… Eldred Huxley.

She typed his name into the search box at the top of the screen and received several hits - the same information she'd found on the two other search engines she'd used. The links included a birth certificate, a number of fines and liens, and even a DUI arrest. The man in the mug shot had intense eyes, familiar eyes, the eyes in the photos she'd found in the garment box with the suit.

But there was something else so damn familiar about those eyes. She was sure she'd seen this man, perhaps in a newspaper or segment on TV about the manner of his death?

She couldn't shake the annoying thought away and was even more frustrated at the lack of a death certificate. There was no mention of the event Kim had described in any of the local newspapers, and nothing in the Heather police blotter.

Obviously, they wouldn't mention Gwendolyn's name since she was a minor at the time, but surely a confrontation that had ended in death would have been documented in some fashion?

But there was simply… nothing.

Sam had related to Charlie the uneasy history of the house as soon as the first ghostly tantrum had occurred. Charlie was initially confused – God, who wouldn't be? - but finally accepted the idea that Eldred Huxley's spirit still inhabited the old house. It sounded insane… but it certainly wasn't the craziest thing happening here.

She'd floated an idea, a suggestion, really… why not pack up all necessities - mainly Charlie's journals and the root ball of the rosebush from the garden outside - and they could find a small cabin somewhere in the middle of nowhere where they could live out the rest of their unconventional relationship shielded from critical judgement and prying eyes.

They certainly had the money. At least, for now. Sam had accepted Arkham Flowers' offer, depositing the sizable check she'd received for transferring exclusive ownership of Blue Charlie and his clippings to them. There'd been a stab of guilt over it. She'd already noted how ubiquitous Blue Charlie was through the garden and the lawn of the backyard when she'd accepted Eric and Rick's deal.

She had the beginning of a plan that included her and Charlie disappearing and hiding out, cashing that check even though she knew anyone interested in the blue rose's clippings would have ample access to them in short time. In fact, Sam was more than a little worried she'd set loose some kind of noxious plant in Washington State, based on how quickly the rose bush was spreading.

Focus. The money is the important part right now.

She figured they could even leave Kim enough money to take care of the damage they'd caused to the rental. Sam didn't want to leave her landlord high and dry.

Charlie had nodded, contemplating the idea, mulling it over, his eyes never leaving hers. Everything was happening so quickly. It was no wonder he was perpetually confused. She wanted to get them both somewhere that would jump start his memories.

But she wasn't kidding herself. She knew there was a fairytale quality to the idea of disappearing together. And fairytales rarely came true.

They'll come after us. The scientists. The religious nut jobs.

Certainly the police.

And then the doorbell rang.

Sam's head jerked up at the sound, her eyes roving the ceiling again for any hint that Charlie was moving. Nothing.

Yet.

The doorbell chimed again, somehow even louder this time.

"For fuck's sake," Sam said, standing and grimacing with the pain. "No."

She rushed painfully back into the living room, trying to keep her anger at bay.

A standing floor lamp suddenly toppled to the floor right in front of her, narrowly missing her head. Huxley's ghost was taunting her, teasing her.

She froze in place, fighting a scream, waiting for something more, a book perhaps, one of the last still remaining in the bookshelf, flying at top speed and striking her ribs or maybe her face with unerring accuracy.

But nothing else happened, and the heavy, urgent knock from the door got Sam moving again, her anger at Kim cutting through her pain. She marched to the door and yanked it open.

"Listen," she hissed, "You're my landlord, okay? Not my -"

On the outside stoop stood an attractive, slightly trashy woman in her early thirties. She had big red hair and was sizing Sam up, visibly unhappy.

"Are you Samantha?" the woman asked.

Sam opened the door a little wider, tied her robe a little tighter. "Yes…" she said, caught off guard. "And you are..?"

"You tell Terry enough is enough," the woman said. "He's had his fun and it's time to come home!"

Sam's mind raced, trying to make sense of the demand, flop sweat breaking on her brow at the mention of Terry's name. "I don't know what you're -"

"Cut the shit," the woman interrupted, peering past Sam into the dim house. "I know he's in there."

"I think maybe you have the wrong place."

The woman focused on Sam, scrutinizing her, how tired she looked, the razor thin scratches covering her arms and neck. She wasn't impressed. "Look, honey," she said, "I don't know what Terry told you, or maybe he said he was in love with you or whatever, but he probably didn't mention he was married, did he?"

Sam eyes grew wide. *Fuck. No, he did not. Fuck, fuck, fuck.*

"I…" she stammered. "Uh, you're…"

"Right. I'm his fucking wife. And you think you're the side chick or something? Honey, you are just one of *many*."

Sam, who was definitely not thinking she was Terry's side chick, kept her mouth shut.

"Yeah, we have an *arrangement*," the woman continued, then leaned to the side and shouted into the house, "But it doesn't allow for being gone for a week, fuckface!"

From the corner of her eye, Sam saw movement. For a moment, she thought it must be Charlie *and what the fuck did he think he was doing?* He was going to ruin everything.

But no. A book from the nearest bookshelf was trembling, *fidgeting*, slipping towards the edge of the shelf. Had it been bumped by one of the strange, spiky vines of the rosebush that was taking over the house?

No. Sam suspected that Spirit Huxley was up to more of his childish bullshit. The book was too far for her to reach without leaving the front door unattended, and Sam had no intention of giving this weirdo a chance to enter the house.

But if this nut job hears that book fall, she'll barge right in…

"Okay." Sam kept her voice calm. "I don't know what's going on with you guys, but it has nothing to do with me. So, good luck and good -"

A switch flipped in the woman's brain, and she snarled, full tilt boogie. "I said cut the shit, bitch!"

Jesus, Sam thought, fear rising in her. *She's just like Terry. These two were a perfect match for each other.*

"His car is right fucking there," the woman continued, pointing at a white, late model Camry parked at the curb a few houses down.

Ah, fuck.

A grim reality set in, and Sam realized that her reunion with Charlie was in sudden and serious peril. But she had no intention of giving up what she'd finally won. Not now, and not ever again.

"Look," she said, attempting to quietly match the woman's intensity, "We met for dinner, yes. I didn't know he was married, but I do know he was a massive asshole, and I left him at the restaurant, okay? I don't know why his car is down there, but I assure you he is not in this house."

The woman glared at Sam. "I believe every single word of that, actually," she said, "Except for the part where he isn't here."

Sam made a point of keeping eye contact with the woman, but in her periphery she could see the trembling book continuing to move, inching closer to the edge of the shelf, slowly, slowly... Christ, this asshole ghost was seriously fucking with her right now.

She was about to push the lie a little further when Terry's wife reached into her pocket. There was a moment of genuine panic -

this fucking nut job is going to shoot me

- but what the woman removed was a cell phone, which she brandished in front of Sam.

The screen showed a topographical map image of streets, woods, houses, and a blinking blue dot over what Sam realized was an aerial view of her new home.

"I track his phone, bitch," the woman said, "and his phone is right… *here.*"

And then the woman pressed a button and showed Sam the screen again. It was a circular photo of Terry, that handsome asshole, and a little bubble underneath that read, "calling".

She got a sudden, clear image of the phone's radio wave racing through the air up into the sky, bouncing off a cell tower or maybe a satellite twenty thousand miles up, then careening back towards Terry's phone, tucked in the jacket his headless corpse was still wearing, and ringing under the dirt and mud of Charlie's Garden.

Would the signal reach the phone? She couldn't see why not. She could imagine the device lighting up in the darkness, startling a worm or maggot that was feasting on Terry's flesh even now.

Holding her breath, she wondered if they'd be able to hear the phone from this far away. That might complicate the situation. Several panicked, ugly thoughts raced through her head and she was horrified by what she might be willing to do to keep her love safe.

But they heard nothing over the shuffling and squawking of the crows outside, and the phone call went to voice message on the woman's phone. She thumbed it off.

Sam said nothing, but she was keenly aware of the movement of the book, just out of reach, still creeping on its own, ready to topple from the bookshelf at any second.

If the woman noticed Sam's anxiety, she must have attributed it to her own presence, and her eyes roamed over the scratches and cuts on Sam's throat.

"I get it," she huffed, "He's fun. He's exciting. His dick has an elbow. You're white bread, so he must seem exotic to you, but he's just another fuckface, and he belongs to me."

And then that book finally fell, a soft thud that both women heard. Sam held her breath, adrenaline flooding her system.

Fight or flight, bitch

Terry's wife sneered. She spoke *around* Sam again, to the dim living room beyond. "That's right, fuckface! Time's up. You had your fun, now get your ass back home. The rent's due! And Catfish wants to borrow the truck! You promised you'd help him move, remember?"

She turned back to Sam. "Okay?" she hissed.

Sam nodded once, her lips tight.

"Good," the woman said, turning on her heels and storming past the crow sentinels lining the fence. They scattered as she approached, then settled back on their perches once she'd passed.

Sam closed the door, locking both the doorknob and the bolt. She stood silent for a moment, her heart hammering in her chest.

A floorboard creaked upstairs, and she wondered how much of the conversation Charlie had heard.

She headed upstairs and peeked into the open bedroom doorway.

"Hey," she said, but did not finish her thought. The bed was a mess of twisted, bloody sheets, but it, like the rest of the room, was empty.

The bathroom had been dark when she walked past it, and that left only the home darkroom she had created for Charlie to be in, unless he had somehow snuck downstairs during her conversation with Terry's wife.

His widow, you mean.

Charlie stood at the darkroom window that overlooked the front yard. He'd pulled aside the blanket that covered it so he could watch the woman leave, and he turned to Sam when she entered. The look on his face was unfamiliar to her, cold, emotionless.

"She might see you," Sam said, striding to the window and pinning the blanket back up, blocking out the light.

Charlie stared at her through the multiple hanging rolls of film she'd developed, photos of Blue Charlie's face and eyes, his fingers, the musculature of his chest and his arms.

She searched his eyes, but they were as unreadable as ever.

2

She approached Charlie carefully, brandishing a set of curved and wickedly sharp professional grade hand clippers.

The rose bush man was lounging in the bathtub, the brackish water cold and cloudy from the custom mix of nitrogen, potassium and phosphorous Sam had sprinkled when she'd drawn the bath.

A few small, sky-blue roses floated on top of the water surrounding Charlie, and he swished a hand gently through them, his skin sucking up the swirling nutrients.

He sipped on the gin and tonic Sam had made at his mimed request. It bothered her, for some reason. She'd never enjoyed the taste of gin, a commonality they'd shared when Charlie was alive. Coming back had changed him in a multitude of ways, it seemed. He was annoyed with her choice of music now, and when she'd tried to pull him up to slow dance with her in the living room, he'd responded by shaking his head, visibly irritated.

She'd also brought him several of his leather notebooks full of sketches and scribbles in his distinctive hand, every word written in blocky, capital letters. Sam had always wondered if this was somehow a manifestation of the passion he felt while writing, as if his thoughts were also in loud, capital letters.

Charlie had raised a bristly eyebrow at the notebooks. "Maybe this will jog some memories," she'd explained. But he'd only skimmed through the first notebook, giving it a quick glance before dropping it on the floor next to the others.

Where was that passion now? Sam tried to push her frustration with the situation away, but Charlie was no closer to remembering his prior life - *their life together* - and seemed uninterested in ever regaining those memories.

She slid a short stool next to the tub and bent her knees with a grimace until she was sitting upon it.

Clacking the hand pruners together twice, she examined several of the thicker suckers that had sprouted from Charlie's shoulders and head, replete with tiny green buds.

Ironic, she thought, *Charlie is growing stronger and healthier every day. And I am utterly wrecked. This love is killing me.*

She got to work, pruning the canes down flush to his wooden skin, dropping small clippings and fully formed roses into the water Charlie was soaking in.

"He's getting worse," Sam murmured as she cut and clipped.

The gin and tonic paused halfway to his mouth, and his strange eyes turned towards her. She had a brief moment of déjà vu, and then it was gone.

"The ghost," Sam elaborated. "Huxley. I thought for sure that woman this morning was going to force her way in when she heard him acting up."

Charlie placed the tumbler on the lip of the bathtub, nodding. He lifted both hands, fists against each other, and mimed a snapping motion, his smile cruel.

Sam couldn't hide her shock. Was he talking about breaking the ghost? Or the woman? "No," she said. "God, no. There's been too much death in this house."

Really? A flush of shame climbed her cheeks as she remembered her own desperate thoughts this morning.

Charlie shrugged, scooping water up and over his chest, and Sam watched it drip down his wooden frame, escaping through the invisible seams where each piece of him met.

"She'll be back. Maybe with the police. She's tracked Terry's phone to the house. I can't believe I didn't realize his car must be somewhere close, too."

She clipped another cane growing from his head, then leaned in to make eye contact. "We should leave," she whispered. "Tonight. I can pick up anything we need, and we'll just go. Get away from the energy in this house, this negativity, all of this shit. We can use your dad's old place outside of Manson until we figure out something more permanent."

Charlie studied her face, his weird, wooden eyes impossible to read. She was sure he was going to turn down the idea, but after a moment, he nodded.

Sam exhaled, relieved, and the pruners snapped together, sharp and loud as she severed a thick cane from his shoulder.

"Oh," she said, startled. "Sorry about-"

Seizing her wrist in one strong, thorny hand, Charlie twisted it fiercely until the pruners dropped to the floor next to his notebooks.

His eyes were cold and cruel and so unlike Charlie's eyes when he was alive. *When he was human.* They drilled into her own, and fear flooded over her, real and primal.

"Ow," she whimpered. "Charlie! You're hurting me!"

He kept the pressure up for a moment longer, the thin, bristly thorns on his hands piercing the flesh of her wrist. His baleful eyes did not leave hers, but he finally released his grip.

Sam jerked away, massaging her sore, bloody wrist. "I'm sorry," she said.

The wooden man stared at her for a moment, then nodded, picking up his gin and tonic and taking a drink from it.

She rose, pain lancing through her midsection. "I'll run to the store," she said when it passed. "Get everything we need for a while. We can leave tonight."

Charlie's eyes narrowed, suspicious, and he lifted himself from the tub, the water cascading from his body, but Sam put a hand on his shoulder, stopping him.

"Don't be silly," she said, smiling through the pain. "We can't risk someone seeing you during the day. You don't exactly blend in. But if we leave as soon as it gets dark, we can be settled in Manson by late this evening."

The mirror over the sink wobbled, then shattered, splintered shards raining into the sink.

Sam's eyes blazed angrily as she looked up. "Yeah," she hissed. "He doesn't like that." She turned to the rest of the house, addressing Huxley's ghost. "You don't like that, do you? You don't like us leaving you to this shitty house all by yourself!"

Charlie reached out, tugging on her robe. She turned back to him and he nodded, motioning her to get moving.

Sam beamed and hurried off to the bedroom to change into real clothes.

"I'll be back in an hour," she called over her shoulder. "Two at the most!"

Alone now, Blue Charlie soaked in the dark, cold water, the living wood that formed his body absorbing the cloudy nourishment of the potassium and nitrogen swirling about him. It soothed him and threatened to put him to sleep.

His memories had trickled back, but he was still struggling to fathom the situation he'd newly been born into.

He'd come to terms with the fact that he'd been dead. And for years, even. And now, in this strange, wooden form, he was somehow alive again. The woman, Samantha, certainly was an interesting wrinkle, and maybe even the entire reason behind his resurrection, but -

A ripple in the water between his legs interrupted his thoughts. A small hand broke the surface of the water, the flesh pale and shriveled, the pink polish on each nail chipped and cracked.

Charlie grasped the fingers within his own gnarled hand and smiled, squeezing it tenderly.

After a moment, the small girl's hand dipped back under the water, and he felt it begin to stroke and tug at him.

He responded by spreading his legs wider and leaning his head against the back edge of the tub as that hand continued to work him skillfully, expertly, exactly the way he had taught her...

෨෬

The front door opening at the house down the street caught Michelle's attention, sending the crows perched on the eaves and fences into a chaotic flurry of caws and squawks and flapping wings.

She lowered herself in her driver's seat, taking a long drag from her smoke and watched the woman - *Samantha* - turn and lock the door, then rush past the shrieking, bobbing crows to her car, a white Subaru.

Ugh, Michelle thought. *Lesbian much?*

She'd had the house under surveillance from her little Toyota for the last few hours, waiting for Terry to show his face, but Samantha was the only movement she'd seen.

What the fuck, Terry? You got her running your errands now?

She'd immediately and grudgingly recognized how pretty the woman was, but whatever kinky shit she and Terry had been up to for the past several days had clearly taken its toll on her.

Terry was a freak. A perv. It was one of the things she loved about him. But the tiny cuts Michelle had seen all over Samantha didn't seem like his usual thing. He wasn't a cutter.

He liked to hit.

And Michelle didn't actually mind getting hit. She saw it as a badge of honor, her ability to take a punch. As long as it wasn't in the face. Her eyes were the money maker, and they were off limits.

After her last fight with Terry, Michelle had driven all the way to Sunset, where she had drunk herself silly, sang karaoke until her throat was raw, and hooked up with a big man named Don Johnson, which she thought was hilarious. She couldn't wait to tell her friends she had fucked Don Johnson.

But he'd turned out to be a gun nut and quite a bit more white trash than she was comfortable with. Still, he served his purpose for the two days she required.

When she'd come back home though, Terry's car was gone. Not surprising... they had a routine. But when he hadn't answered his phone or come home after a couple days, her fury became a living thing, growing by leaps and bounds.

After several attempts, Michelle was able to get into his dating account. His password was the same one he'd been using for the last ten years for everything, and once in, she'd started snooping.

The dating profile was chuckle-worthy. He'd listed himself as six feet tall and a hundred and eighty-five pounds, magically adding an inch to his height and shearing fifteen pounds from his weight.

But the eye-rolling detail was the relationship status he'd toggled as "single." He couldn't give her the respect of an "it's complicated", at least?

As suspected, Terry had gone fishing for a hook-up as soon as she'd left the house, and he'd connected with several in no time.

Michelle had scowled at how attractive Samantha was, even in the silly dating profile photo she'd uploaded. Jealousy came easily to her, and she typed Samantha's name into her phone's browser, finding a brand-new address for the woman. The same address Terry's phone was last pinged at.

She'd hoped to find Terry sneaking out after the confrontation this morning, but that hadn't happened, infuriating Michelle even further. What the fuck was he waiting for? It didn't matter. The woman's departure meant that Terry was in the house alone, now.

She reckoned it might just be time to pay Terry a little visit inside that house.

But before she could act on the thought, the door of the neighboring house had opened as well, and an older hippie woman stepped out, as if she'd also been waiting for Samantha to leave. She hurried across the sidewalk and through the gate to the other yard, the numerous crows observing her warily.

The neighbor glanced furtively both ways, and Michelle lowered herself deeper into her car, though she thought it must be nearly impossible to be seen at this distance. Then the woman produced a key and let herself in, swiftly closing the door behind her.

Michelle's eyes narrowed as she sat back up in her seat, shaking her head. Her cocksucker of a husband had really outdone himself this time.

Getting a little side action on your side action, Terry? You fucking turd.

Kim gently closed the door behind her, shutting out the cawing of the crows and waiting for her eyes to adjust to the dim light of the living room.

The smell hit her first, stenchy, earthy and floral, and… *moist.*

Her heart was thumping furiously, but she ignored it and set her jaw. She wasn't comfortable breaking into her renter's home, but there was something going on over here that Samantha wasn't telling her. Kim thought it might have something to do with the fucking garden in the back yard. She turned her gaze to the ceiling.

Or the bathtub.

But something else was also going on. The loud shouting of the woman who'd arrived this morning left no doubt. What had Samantha gotten herself involved in?

The state of the living room shocked Kim. The place was a wreck, books scattered all over the floor, cracked glass in picture frames, furniture toppled. A marked contrast to the tidy space she'd seen only a week or so ago.

It looked like a crime scene.

Or a giant temper tantrum.

The hell you doing to my house, girl?

She took another step into the room, then stopped, keenly aware of a sound, a constant, muted shuffling that made her think of wind through tall grass, or leaves falling from a tree.

The sound led her to a bookshelf, its contents spilled to the floor, and she peered into the darkness, seeing nothing.

But then, movement. Kim took a step backwards, sure she was dealing with bugs at the back of the shelf, a nest of spiders or cockroaches.

Pulling out her cell phone, she aimed its bright screen into the shadows at the rear of the bookshelf, trying to puzzle out the details of what she was seeing.

One of my gift baskets, was her first thought.

Or part of one. She could see the intricate weave of the basket in the phone's light, but just as her screen timed out and plunged the back of the shelf into darkness, she saw something else.

A flex.

The weave of the basket seemed to *shift*, and then all of those thin strands of wood pulsed, squeezing and moving as one…

Growing.

This time she toggled on the phone's flashlight, heartbeat thudding in her ears, and she turned the bright beam back towards the shelf.

In the sharper light she could see that the back of the shelf – indeed, all of the shelves – were overlayed with long, bristly rose vines and blue buds, and the noise she heard – *an impossible noise* - was the sound of those vines sliding against each other as they moved.

They had slipped through a seam at the shelf, invading and advancing under the living room's wallpaper.

She reached out and touched the wall, feeling the extruded edges of the vines under the old wallpaper. Fingers light against the surface, she walked, tracing the vines back into the kitchen, her eyes going wide at the sight of the room.

The rose vines and canes sprouted from every seam, every opening. They spilled from the heater grate, from the sink's faucet and drain, even from the electrical outlets.

Kim's eyes were drawn to the cracked window over the sink and the garden outside, shocked at the growth of the blue rosebush along the fence. Hairline cracks marred the concrete patio, the footing buckling from the sudden and massive growth spurt of the roots as it claimed the house.

And up the stairwell, Kim realized, afraid now of what it might lead her to up there.

She crept back through the living room, climbing the gloomy stairwell cautiously, pausing when one step betrayed her with a loud groan.

You watched her leave. There's no one in the house.

Still, she continued to move softly up the stairs and through the dim hallway. This kind of intrusion demanded silence.

What are you afraid of? A ghost?

But she could admit that she *was* afraid. A presence, an energy, filled the space here, surpassing the mere echoes of the house's dreadful past.

She glanced through the bathroom's open door as she passed, unwilling to go inside. The only source of light in the darkness were a few flickering tea lights, the very ones she had included in the housewarming gift basket she brought over for Samantha when she moved in.

The bathtub looked like it had water in it, and that was enough to raise the hair on her arms. She'd be damned if she was going to investigate that further. Her actions had already left lasting echoes and indelible marks that were not easily exorcised from her own memories.

We are all haunted houses, she thought, remembering a snippet of a poem she'd read in high school. She quickened her step.

Samantha had taken the bigger bedroom as her own, and it seemed to have avoided the downstairs hurricane that had tossed and turned the kitchen and living room. The bed appeared disheveled, but Kim gave it little thought. She rarely made her own bed these days.

Down the hallway beckoned the second bedroom

Gwendolyn's bedroom

which, although dark, seemed to be illuminated by a dim, red light.

Kim stopped at the threshold of the smaller bedroom, taking in the sight.

She had enough common sense to recognize a darkroom when she saw one. But she wasn't prepared for the stench of sulfur or the unspooled rolls of film hanging from wires stretched from wall to wall.

A dark red bulb had been screwed into the standard light socket in the ceiling, and it barely illuminated the room. Kim expected to see some full-size photographs soaking in the trays full of chemicals, but they were empty.

A part of her brain realized there would have to be a machine of some kind to make prints from these smaller images, and that was something unlikely to be found in a homemade darkroom like this.

The décor of the room threw Kim off. The last time she'd spent any time here she'd collected Gwendolyn's personal effects, bagging her clothes, books, and toys for delivery to the dump.

She shook the thought away and strode to the darkened window, pulling away the thick blanket that was secured against it.

Sunlight streamed into the room and Kim held her breath, half expecting the dangling rolls of film to all turn black. When that didn't happen, she exhaled, relieved, and chided herself for not understanding anything about the process.

Who uses film to take pictures anymore anyway?

In the light from the window, the details in the photos finally became visible to her, drawing her closer to examine them.

There was Samantha's prize rosebush. Kim still didn't understand the significance of a slightly different looking, natural blue rose, and one that had been spliced, but she could appreciate that it was a beautiful flower, even though it seemed to be taking over her rental property. And here was a photo of that creepy fucking scarecrow. Even in this tiny image, Kim could identify the craftsmanship in Samantha's photos. There was something about the angles and the lighting that Kim recognized was a talent that she did not possess herself. Yes, Samantha had a real camera and Kim had an iPhone, but Samantha knew how to compose a shot, how to capture something that a regular cell phone camera user could not.

On the next hanging roll of film, Kim paused, unsure of what she was looking at.

What the fuck is that?

It was… what? A tree? A bush? A plant of some kind. Yeah, a rose bush. There were those gorgeous blue petals, but they were emerging from tiny buds and -

WHAT THE FUCK IS THAT?

- they were on a face, a fucking wooden face, that was unmistakably a face made from all the stalks and canes of a tightly coiled rosebush. There were cheekbones and lips and teeth and then, in this next photo a *tongue*, a fucking wooden tongue covered in tiny bristles and striations, and this wasn't some weird art installation. These pictures weren't taken outside. They were here, in this house, in the bedroom with the messy bed, and there was adoration in them, and awe, and *motion,* a lifelike realism that made Kim incredibly uncomfortable.

She felt compelled to examine the other rolls of film hanging from the wire, and on this one, she discovered the creature's eyes. The eyeballs of this thing, flat and woody, like snipped rose canes, full of grain and fiber. But… real. Alive. And as she studied the photos of this monster's eyes, she realized they were also familiar.

Horribly familiar.

"No," Kim whispered, bringing a hand to her mouth. "No fucking way."

She grabbed the rolls of film, squinting at them through the daylight streaming through the window.

Abomination was the word that lodged in Kim's mind. Whatever the creature was, it just did not belong.

Breath coming in short, uncontrollable bursts, Kim backed away from the photos, horror and fear flooding her senses. She turned to leave the room, to flee the house, to get help…

And Blue Charlie was standing there, still moist and dripping from the tub.

He reached a gnarled, thorny hand towards Kim, yanking her by the throat and pulling her close until their faces were only inches apart. He opened his mouth, and a woody, bristly rasp emerged.

"*Kiiiiim,*" he said.

Kim's eyes widened from the grip, her scream cut short. She recognized that voice, even through the dirt and twigs and leaves that made up his new vocal cords.

৪০০৪

Sam pulled her jacket a little tighter to herself as she pushed the cart through the aisles of Williford's Supermarket.

She'd grabbed one with a wobbly wheel, loud and screechy, but she suspected that wasn't why the other shoppers she passed gave her such odd looks. She must appear more miserable than ever under the unforgiving fluorescent lights of the store, her flesh crisscrossed with multiple scratches and bruises. Blood continued to seep from the punctures on her wrist Charlie had made earlier.

It must appear as if she were stocking up for another pandemic, or a long, cold winter. She'd filled the cart with canned foods, bottled water and toilet paper. Everything she thought they'd need to hide away for a while.

Hobbling along, she pushed the cart into the pharmacy section. She paused and examined a wall of first aid products. From the shelf she pulled several small boxes of band-aids and antibiotic ointment, dropping them into the cart and following them with bandages and injury wraps. This promised to be her new fashion statement.

The cart's wheel squealed as she left the pharmacy section, and she abruptly halted, considering several small boxes near an end cap.

Sam grimaced, resigned to her fate, and grabbed one of the small cartons of KY personal lube. After a moment, she grabbed another half-dozen cartons, dropping them all into the cart.

From the pharmacy she crossed the entire store to get to the gardening section of Williford's. It was only one short aisle containing packaged seeds, plastic watering cans, and a few small bags of inexpensive potting soil, but Sam didn't have the time or energy to head over to Morgret & Sons again, and she thought she might find what she needed here.

And there it was, a medium-sized, pink and yellow bag of Captain Zamora's Rose Food, a proprietary blend of fish emulsion, composted tea and bone meal.

Charlie had sworn by it for the rose that bore his name, and now that he had *become* Blue Charlie, Sam thought a bath of this once they got to Manson might put him in a better mood.

The bag went in the cart, and she limped it towards the front of the store.

She unloaded the contents onto the register's conveyor belt, and the young cashier rang everything up, bagging them as he went.

He paused in the middle of ringing up the metric ton of bandages and ointment, and Sam could feel the heat climbing her face as he took in the cuts and scratches covering her skin. She refused to make eye contact.

"Ma'am," he said softly, and she finally looked up. His eyes were too kind for his young age. "Is everything okay? Do you need me to call somebody?"

She smiled, the exhaustion and madness abruptly catching up to her. For the briefest moment she considered telling the boy that everything was definitely *not* okay, but she didn't know who he could call to help her with the decapitated corpse buried in her garden, or the endless harassment by the neighborhood crows, or the aggressive ghost that was haunting her house, or the fact that sex with her resurrected husband was tearing apart her insides.

A humorless chuckle escaped her lips and she said, "I'm fine," and his smile was sad. No one was fooling anyone today, but he resumed bagging the last of her items.

She slid her card into the card reader. "What's the maximum amount of cash I can withdraw?"

ഇൗരൂ

Michelle's patience had worn through. After fifteen minutes of no activity, it was time to act.

This is the way you want to play it, Terry?

She leaned over and unlatched the Toyota's glove box.

Maybe it's time for a little Come-to-Jesus talk.

Fishing through a bunch of receipts, napkins, and a pair of sunglasses, Michelle pulled out a snub nosed .38, a little purse gun she'd bought off a dude she'd been fucking on and off for years. She might not approve of the veritable arsenal Don Johnson was keeping in his trailer in Sunset, but that didn't mean she didn't know how to take care of herself. Flipping open the cylinder, she briefly entertained the idea of removing the bullets. She wanted to scare them, not kill them.

Still, if this new hippie chick tried something, Michelle didn't want to regret going in with an empty gun.

She snapped the cylinder shut and tucked the gun into her waistband.

Exiting the car, she hurried to the house, head on a swivel. The last thing she needed now was some nosy neighbor peeking through their curtains and seeing her sneaking around the place.

This time, the crows appeared more agitated with her, as if they could sense that the stakes had been raised by the gun in her waistband. She paid them no heed.

Michelle darted around the side of the house, glancing through the windows, but the blinds were closed and she could see nothing. Peering over the fence, she saw the backyard was overgrown with wild roses, exploding from the edge of a patio and climbing up the side of the house. She decided that entering through the front door was her best option.

Checking her surroundings one last time, she crept up the stoop to the front door and tried the knob. It turned easily and she opened the door.

She leaned her head through the doorway, pausing for just a beat, then went inside.

The house was dark, silent, and she closed the door softly behind her, waiting for her eyes to adjust to the gloom.

The place smelled fragrant, funky, like a greenhouse. But it was the condition of the living room that stopped her in her tracks.

Terry and Michelle had dabbled in molly-fueled fuckfests before, where they would both take copious amounts of the drug and watch a ton of porn while they fucked their way across the house. It left the place in shambles, clothes strewn everywhere, half-empty water bottles littering the floor.

But whatever he was up to with these chicks was obviously a good deal weirder.

Books all over the floor, rugs peeled back, even a broken lamp…

Shit, these chicks are freaky…

The downstairs was silent and empty, so Michelle snuck up the stairwell, pausing when she hit a creaky step, but moving on when it became apparent that she hadn't been detected yet.

At the top of the stairs she listened for any movement, and when she heard none she crept down the dim hallway towards the open bedroom door at the end.

She walked past the darkened bathroom, oblivious to the darker, heavier shadow within. Nor did she notice the bloody smear that ran along the carpet from the bedroom at the end of the hallway.

Michelle paused at the doorway, confused. There was a shape on the bed, obviously a person, but where was Terry?

And then her heart skipped a beat, because the figure on the bed was the woman she'd seen entering the house a little earlier… and she was unmistakably dead. Someone had left her face and throat slashed beyond repair, torn to ribbons, and the sheets soaked with her blood.

Michelle gasped, covering her mouth with her hand. She moved closer, her thoughts racing frantically. Where was Terry? Had he done this? No. He could get violent, but murder? No way. But even as she tried to deny it, she remembered how frightened she'd been multiple times in the past, when his drinking and his temper got the best of him.

The dead woman's eyes were wide and unseeing, and Michelle fought the wave of nausea that rushed over her.

Don't faint. Don't faint.

"Fuck," she whispered. Her gaze flicked to every corner of the room, and she was relieved to find it empty. Still, it was time to get out of this house. Terry had gotten himself involved in something much darker than he intended, she was sure, and she wanted no part of it.

As she turned to leave though, the dead woman jerked into a sitting position.

Michelle stifled a scream, terrified, but took a step towards the woman, arms outstretched to steady her.

"Oh, Jesus," Michelle said, "Hold on, don't move. You're hurt. Bad."

The woman stood, wobbling a bit, then turned her torn-up face towards Michelle. Her dazed eyes struggled to focus, and when she spoke, it seemed as though she were speaking *past* Michelle.

"You ruined her face," the woman said.

A chill ran down Michelle's spine. The woman in front of her was undeniably in her late 50's. Probably older. But the voice that came from her was that of a young girl, a teenager at most.

Michelle stared blankly at her, fear and horror gripping her in their tight embrace, rooting her to the floor.

The older woman staggered towards her and that eerie, little girl's voice came from her mouth again. "I don't want this one," she said, petulant. "She's old and you ruined her face!"

Michelle reached out to help support her, but the woman pushed her away and Michelle lost her balance, arms pinwheeling as she stumbled backwards.

Into the arms of a nightmare.

It was humanoid, man-sized, but made of spiky, wooden skin. As he grabbed Michelle, she felt dozens of thin, thorny vines erupt from his hands, wrapping around her head and face like the tentacles of an octopus, forcing their way down her open mouth, sawing against her flesh as they tightened.

And the last thing she heard was that little girl's frantic voice: "No! She's pretty! Don't fuck up her face!"

∞⃝⃝

The sky above her new home was a beautiful oil painting of purple and orange as Sam pulled back into the driveway, and she had a moment of regret that she'd never gotten the chance to love the place, to enjoy it and take advantage of what it had to offer.

We'll do it somewhere else. That's all that matters.

The rear hatch window of the Subie was blocked by all of the grocery bags she'd jammed into the back of the car. There was still enough space for a couple of suitcases and, of course, space for Blue Charlie's original root ball. She hoped the severe pruning they'd have to do to free the rosebush from the house would not do any permanent damage to the plant.

The sight of a single, small blue rose popping up through a buckled fissure of her old, asphalt driveway interrupted her thoughts. In the span of a week, Blue Charlie had crept underground from the tiny backyard garden all the way to the front of the house. He must have wound his way into the vacant lot by now, and probably on Kim's side of the fence, as well.

The owners of Arkham Flowers would be furious. She'd have to withdraw as much cash as possible in the coming week or two. As soon as they realized the rose was widely accessible to everyone, they would dispute the contract.

When she stepped out of the car she paused, stunned, her focus no longer on the flower.

Crows covered the entire run of the wood fence, every spare inch occupied by their large, black-feathered bodies. Their heads bobbed and they fidgeted from one leg to the other, cawing occasionally. They scrutinized the house intently.

Her eyes widened as she realized it wasn't just the fence. The big black birds covered the telephone wires above her, as well.

The branches of the trees surrounding the house were alive with shifting and stretching crows, all jostling for more space.

And the house itself. Every eave, every gutter, every open space... there were literally hundreds upon hundreds of the birds crowding her home.

Sam cautiously moved through the yard, anticipating the birds swarming and attacking her. They shrieked and flapped their wings but kept their distance, and she reached the front door with only her nerves rattled.

Captivated by the birds' behavior, she didn't give a thought to opening the door without her key.

She entered the house and latched the door behind her, leaning against it and releasing the breath she'd been holding.

Sam's eyes quickly adapted to the dim lighting, and she made a beeline for the kitchen.

"Sorry that took so long," she called out. "But I think we've got everything we need for a couple weeks, at least."

She opened a cupboard, pulled out a canvas shopping bag and began filling it with items. A half-full jar of peanut butter, all of the packages of instant ramen and soy sauce packets she'd survived on since Charlie passed, an unopened box of Saltine crackers.

Removing those items revealed several very thick rose canes along the back of the cupboard, and Sam wondered again how much of the house had been invaded by Blue Charlie's exceptional root ball.

"Did you see all of the birds outside?" she called out, realizing she'd heard nothing from Charlie yet. "It's kind of scary." Her eyes drifted to the ceiling. "Charlie? Are you ready? We should leave as soon as it gets dark!"

Still no response. She left the kitchen, keenly aware of the eerie silence that had settled over the house. It was as if the hundreds of crow bodies outside had buffered and insulated the home from all other sound.

At the bottom of the stairs she paused, peering up into the darkness. "Charlie?"

From upstairs she heard a clumsy *thump*, but instead of reassuring Sam, it sent a jolt of anxiety through her.

Something's wrong.

She climbed each step slowly, the silence of the house oppressive. Why wouldn't he answer her?

"Hey babe," she said. "Everything okay? We need to get going…"

At the landing she turned left, walking past the bathroom, which was empty and dark, save for a few of the tea lights flickering within.

"Charlie? Where are you?"

She stopped at the bedroom, flicking the light switch. The old incandescent bulb flashed and broke, tiny sparks showering from it. The instant of light illuminated the horrific mess on the bed, and Sam saw the twisted sheets, sodden with blood. An impossible amount of blood.

Movement at the corner of the room caught her attention and she turned to find a figure near the closet. Sam recognized Kim's silhouette, but it did little to ease her mind. She cautiously entered the bedroom.

"Kim," she said. "What are you…"

Kim staggered out of the darkness towards Sam, her ruined face and throat the undeniable source of the bloodied sheets.

Horrified at the carnage, Sam rushed to her friend's side, embracing Kim and trying to guide her towards the door and help. "Oh my God," she said, unsure how her friend was even still alive. "Oh my God, hang on, we need to get you to the hospital! Holy shit, Kim! What happened? Where's Charlie?"

She paused, her own words ringing in her head. The gears in her mind were spinning fast now, making horrific connections.

She turned to face her friend. "Kim. Who did this to you? Where's Charlie?"

Kim's eyes, flat and dull, fought to focus and finally succeeded. She tried to push Sam away, struggling to escape her grip, wheezing wetly through her savaged throat.

And when she spoke, it was with the voice of a young girl.

"No," Kim said, "No."

She flung Sam to the bloody bed, towering over her.

"No!" Kim shouted in that unrecognizable voice. "She's not your friend! She was never your friend! She was never *my* friend!"

Sam stared up at her, bewildered.

"She…" Kim stammered, "She *saw* us. She saw my daddy."

And then it clicked with Sam. *This was not Kim.* This was not her friend speaking. Kim was gone, and this thing was wearing her dead body like a suit and using her mouth to speak. The same thing happened with Terry after Charlie had killed him.

And if he had *been able to speak at that time, would it have been with this little girl's voice?*

She was suddenly certain of it.

"You're not Kim…" Sam whispered.

The dead eyes of her friend glared down at her and Sam recoiled.

"…Gwendolyn?"

Kim seemed to stand up straighter at the mention of the name. Her lifeless lips moved again, but it was Gwendolyn's voice that came from them. "She came over. To yell at us."

It took a moment, but Sam realized the girl was talking about Kim, about the day she'd come over and Gwendolyn had accidentally killed her father.

"And daddy… he… he…"

"He tore her shirt," Sam whispered.

Kim nodded. "I was so angry at him," Gwendolyn said. "He was staring at her! At her tits! He wanted to fuck her! I could tell!"

"You hit him with the baseball bat."

"Yes," Gwendolyn huffed. "He fell over. Hurt. I was so scared!"

"It's okay. You did the right thing."

Kim's lip turned up in a snarl. "And I told this old bitch to go home! To get out and to mind her own business!"

"You saved her," Sam said, but she was suddenly uncertain.

Gwendolyn ignored her. "She took the bat! She took the bat from me and she hit daddy in the head again! Over and over until it didn't even look like a head anymore!"

Sam felt the air rush out of her lungs. "…what?"

"She killed daddy! She killed him, then told me he had been hurting me! But he wasn't hurting me! He *loved* me! We were in love!"

"No," Sam said, the room spinning. "No. Your daddy was…"

"And then she made me help her bury him in the garden."

Sam staggered backwards.

No, she thought. *No, no, no…* She'd dug the hole for Blue Charlie in the garden. She'd pounded that scarecrow's garden pole deep into that dirt. She would have found something! She would have felt something!

But she *had* felt something.

In the storm that night, in the pounding rain with the lightning flashing above her, as if nature were angry at what she was attempting, the pole had hit something, had not wanted to go further, but she had pushed on, finally breaking through it with her grief and her tears and her anger and her blood…

Sam tried to push the thoughts away, but they crowded in on her. She could see that pretty teenage girl in the photos from the garment box, standing next to Kim in the garden, tamping down all of the recently displaced dirt and the little sign that said, *Gwendolyn's Garden.*

In her mind's eye, Gwendolyn was silently weeping at that moment, scared, confused. Was Kim also crying?

No, Sam thought. *She definitely wasn't crying, was she? She was one tough broad.*

Sam's thoughts turned abruptly to Greg, Kim's cheating husband, and how he had suddenly died. She suspected it was no accident.

"She put me in the bathtub afterwards," Gwendolyn continued. "Made me clean myself up, and kept telling me the same thing, over and over…"

Now Sam imagined the young girl naked in the tub, knees to her chin in the dirty bath, tears still spilling down her cheeks as Kim squeezed soapy water from a sponge over the girl's blonde hair, rinsing the shampoo out.

"…she kept saying Daddy was going to rape her. Maybe kill her," Gwendolyn said. "She said that Daddy had been hurting me. That he'd been raping me. That I saved her by killing Daddy! *But I wasn't the one who killed him!*"

She had enough of her father's shit, Kim told Sam when she recounted the awful story several nights ago. *She wasn't going to let him hurt anyone else.*

"I told her she was wrong! I told her that my daddy loved me! That we were just waiting to tell everyone until I was older. She didn't like that!"

No, I'll bet she didn't.

"I was so angry! I told her I was going to tell everyone the truth! That my daddy loved me and that she killed him!"

Oh, no. Sam's stomach flipped. *How much worse can this get?* Now she understood why there were no police reports concerning Eldred Huxley's death.

"What did she do," Sam whispered, knowing the answer. "What did she do to you when you said you'd tell everyone?"

"She pushed me under the water! She held me down!"

And Sam could see her doing it, could see Kim, young and strong and suddenly faced with a murder investigation... she could see Kim grab Gwendolyn by that long, blonde hair, pulling her backwards, pushing her head into and under the water.

She struggled to see her friend's kind face during this horrific act. Were Kim's eyes mad with fury while she held the struggling girl down, murdering her in eighteen inches of soapy water?

No, Sam thought. *I think her eyes were colder than a witch's tit in November. I think her eyes were cold, and her lips were tight, and her arms like iron as Gwendolyn grappled and splashed and fought until it all just... finally... stopped.*

Sam shook her head to clear the vision, tears streaming down her cheeks. "Oh God," she whispered. "No. Kim... why. Why."

Gwendolyn glared at Sam through Kim's dead eyes. "Then she cut me up," she said.

Sam's eyes widened.

"And used acid," Gwendolyn continued. "And lime. And just rinsed me down the drain of our own bathtub. It took..." Gwendolyn's voice cracked, and tears sprang from Kim's eyes. "... *days.*"

Sam shook her head at the horror. "And then she bought your house so that no one would ever find out."

A painful sob escaped her lips, a bark that started at her chest, at her heart. Kim turned and faced her again, dead, horrific... smiling.

"And you moved in," Gwendolyn grinned. "Planted your rosebush. And brought daddy back."

Sam sobbed again, her eyes hot and wet, trying to understand what the girl meant. "No…"

Kim's eyes were shiny now, almost alive, the blood on her face black in the darkened room. "You call him Charlie," Gwendolyn said. "But that's not his name. That's not Daddy's name."

Sam staggered, her head spinning, her mind fraying at the edges as the pieces slammed into place. The flying books, the falling pictures, the furniture, the lamp, all of it seemed so silly, so callow, like a child throwing a tantrum… because it *was* a child throwing a tantrum. Gwendolyn was the ghost in the house. And Eldred inhabited the living form of the rose bush. Charlie… *the real Charlie*… had never been anything but a voice in her head.

"No," she said, repeating the word, refusing to believe this horror, the pain and suffering and humiliation she'd endured over the last several days. "No, no, no, no…"

She backed away from Kim, away from the bedroom, but the dead body of her landlord followed her out into the hallway.

"You can't leave," Gwendolyn said. "I don't want this body! Her face is all fucked up! *I want you.*"

Kim grabbed at her, yanking savagely, and they struggled for a moment, locked together.

Sam put a hand in the mess of Kim's face, trying to push the woman away. Blood, muscle, and flesh squished between Sam's fingers, but Kim was unfazed.

"You don't get to leave!"

They waltzed like that across the landing, Sam fighting for dear life, and at the top of the stairs she felt her foot suddenly slip on the edge.

But she threw her tiny frame as hard as she could in the opposite direction, twisting and breaking free of Kim's grasp. The older woman stumbled, arms pinwheeling as she toppled ass over teakettle down the narrow wooden stairs, and she hit the edge of one of those steps with a terrifying *crunch* before tumbling the rest of the way to the bottom and lying still.

Sam stood at the top of the stairs, breath hitching, eyes wide as she stared down at the body of her landlord.

Kim lay motionless on the hardwood floor near the front door, her head visibly dented inward, eyes open but seeing nothing. She was dead. Again.

"Sssaamaaaanthaaa…"

The voice came from right next to her, Blue Charlie gripping her tightly as he forced her name through his dry, thorny vocal cords.

Startled, Sam screamed, struggling to tear away from Charlie -

that's not Charlie it was never *Charlie*

- but his grip was unbreakable.

"Get away from me!"

Eldred Huxley tilted his wooden head towards her, his grin full of malefic glee. He opened his mouth, perhaps to speak again, but a loud thump from outside the house cut him off. Another heavy thump came from above, and then another from the other side of the house.

Sam struggled to break free, and Eldred's weird, wooden eyes darted towards the ceiling at the sounds.

If crows are indeed messengers of the gods, or stealers of souls, or sent by their Queen to protect a princess, perhaps that might explain why they had been drawn to the old house that had somehow trapped poor Gwendolyn Huxley within its walls. And perhaps they had been aware of the powerful grief-magic that Samantha was unwittingly wielding as she planted her rosebush - itself a thing that defied nature - over the rotting corpse of Eldred Huxley, and then watered it with her own blood and tears. And perhaps they instinctively knew to stand guard as that grief fueled the dark and twisted, oblivious sex-rituals occurring inside the house, powered by pain and blood and fear and anger.

But this home must have finally reached a critical level, its walls imprinted with more misery and lust and murder than nature could ever allow, and on some unseen cue the crows had decided there would be no more waiting.

They launched from their perches, from the fence and the trees, wings spread wide, and hurled themselves at the house as one, at its doors and windows, at any point of ingress, wave after wave of their bodies relentlessly thumping against the wood and glass in an attempt to gain entry.

Sam didn't understand the noise she was hearing - to her it sounded as if the house had been caught in a hailstorm of epic proportions - but she took advantage of Eldred's distraction and finally tore free of his piercing grip. But he still blocked the stairway and her means of escape.

Instead, she darted into the bathroom, slamming the door shut and throwing the tiny bolt that locked it, planting her back against the door. The room was shadowy, lit only by the few flickering tea lights.

Outside, the storm continued, the thumping against the house furious and unending, as wave after wave of the ebon birds flung themselves against its doors and windows and gables.

She jumped as a crow slammed against the little window above the bathtub, which she could see was still full of the water Charlie had been soaking in only a few hours ago.

That was Eldred. Not Charlie. It had been Eldred the entire time.

As if on cue, the bathroom door shook in its frame, and she braced herself tighter against it as Eldred slammed upon it from the other side.

Another crow bashed against the bathroom window, cracking it in its frame.

The crows don't like him, she realized. *It had nothing - or little - to do with the rosebush. They didn't like Eldred Huxley being back from the dead.*

Her gaze darted to every corner of the tiny room, looking for anything she could defend herself with.

Nothing. There was absolutely nothing. And when things seemed like they couldn't get any worse...

The dark water in the bathtub rippled, bubbled, and a figure jolted upright, the water pouring from her soaked, red hair. Her face looked like a jigsaw puzzle as she turned to face Sam.

Holy fuck it's that Michelle nut job

Sam screamed, and Huxley's heavy, wooden fists continued to pound on the bathroom door against her back, as the crows hammered relentlessly at the house's exterior.

Terry's dead wife rose from the tub, her hair and clothes streaming water. She caught her dim reflection in the cracked and broken bathroom mirror.

"No, no, no!" Michelle said, but what came out was Gwendolyn's petulant tone again. "This is not okay! What the fuck!"

She spread her arms out as if to say, *Can you believe I have to deal with this shit?* then stepped out of the bathtub, first with one soggy sneaker, and then the other, squishing towards Sam.

Sam pushed herself deeper against the bathroom door, which rattled on its hinges from the blows being rained upon the other side.

Michelle reached out. "Don't worry," she said in that little girl's voice. "I promise I won't fuck up your face."

Sam screamed again but was silenced as the dead woman's hands locked around her throat, squeezing.

Her sanity hung by a thread, but one thought pierced the encroaching madness. *She needs me dead! She can't get inside me while I'm alive!*

But Michelle's fingers around her throat were iron, and Sam couldn't break the grip. The girl was determined, after twenty-five years, to inhabit a proper body.

Using the door as leverage, Sam pushed against Michelle, but the woman was immovable. Her hand slipped and slid down Michelle's waist as stars popped in her vision…

And Sam's eyes widened as she seized the wooden grip of a revolver tucked in the waistband of the dead woman's pants.

Holy shit.

She'd never held a gun, much less fired one. Didn't know where the safety was. Had no idea if it would even work after being underwater.

But she pulled the revolver out and jammed the barrel hard against Michelle's stomach, squeezing the trigger again and again. The gun bucked in her hands, roaring as she put several bullets into Michelle's torso.

The woman staggered backwards, blood blossoming all over her shirt and stomach. She looked up at Sam with a condescending sneer. "I'm already dead you stupid-"

Sam slammed the gun barrel right to Michelle's forehead and squeezed the trigger again. Blood, brains and bone exploded behind the dead woman, and she fell straight backwards, crashing into the tub, feet dangling almost comically over the rim.

Drawing deep, burning breaths through her bruised throat, Sam fumbled with the gun and finally found the cylinder release. She popped it open and groaned as she realized the cylinder held only empty shells. She'd fired every bullet she had and felt like a fool.

The crows continued their assault on the house, the noise a thunderous soundtrack to her failure. There was nothing left to defend herself against Eldred Huxley.

The sound of the crows battering the exterior troubled Huxley on a primal level, but not as much as the six gunshots that had come from inside the bathroom and the deathly silence that now followed.

He paused his assault on the door, placing one wooden ear against it and attempting to block out the sound of the thunder outside.

He could hear nothing else. Had Gwendolyn fired the shots, killing Samantha? He'd miss her. She was just plain fun when it came to the bedroom. Or had Samantha fired the shots, destroying the body of the redhead that Gwendolyn must have possessed?

After a moment, he tapped softly against the door, forcing a word through his still developing vocal cords. "Sssamaaaantha?"

Tilting his head at the silence that followed, he realized what must have transpired. He smiled, his wooden lips curling up wickedly. "Gwendolynnnn…"

Over the sound of the corvid assault on the outside of the house, he heard the tiny bolt lock on the bathroom door slide open.

Huxley reached a bristly hand out, grasping the doorknob and twisting it.

The door unlatched and swung slowly open.

Samantha stood in the doorway, arms stretched towards him. In one hand she held one of the tiny tea lights she'd lit earlier around the bathroom in a worthless romantic gesture. In the other, a purple can of aerosol hairspray.

She aimed a long stream of flaming aerosol at Huxley's face, the hairspray coating his wooden features like a poor man's napalm, sticking to his face, burning his wooden eyes.

"Burn in hell, you fucking creep!"

Huxley threw his hands up, staggering backwards, and Samantha pressed the attack, dropping her makeshift flamethrower and pulling from her waistband the wicked hand clippers she'd left in the bathroom earlier.

With savage fury, she drove the hand clippers into his left eye and Huxley fell to one knee, roaring in pain.

Sam saw her chance. With Huxley blinded, she skirted past him towards the stairs.

But not quickly enough. The wooden man flailed, snagging her forearm in his thorny grip.

Sam wailed in despair and pain, and Huxley dragged her back to his bristly, unyielding frame with a victorious shout.

so close I was so goddamned close…

But she was empty. She had nothing left in her. Her arm - her entire body - screamed in agony, her insides so cruelly torn and shredded over the last week, and she slumped, the fight taken out of her. She welcomed whatever solace death might afford her.

And then all hell broke loose.

The bathroom window, subjected to so many blows from the crows outside, finally shattered, and the hallway erupted with dozens of black-feathered bodies, and then hundreds, funneling through that tiny window, all of them shrieking and cawing, flapping and attacking with relentless fury, every single one of them intent on the destruction of Eldred Huxley's abominable, wooden body.

They dove at him, shredding and ripping and tearing at his wood skin, and all the while their numbers increased, every single one of the black birds outside finding that point of entry and streaming into the house, ready and willing to sacrifice themselves to insure the obliteration of this blight upon the natural order.

But Eldred Huxley refused to budge. One sharp and unforgiving hand clenched around Sam's flayed forearm, the other swinging wildly and connecting constantly, sending dozens of shattered crow bodies to the floor. The hand clippers jutted from his left eye like the defiant rosebud in the driveway outside.

Sam struggled weakly against him, his grip like a saw blade, but it was all she could do to withstand the furious tornado of black feathers that whipped around them both, ripping and tearing at her own skin as well.

By sheer force of weight and mass, the crow army pushed and pressed the two of them to the top of the steps, to the *edge* of the steps, and then Eldred and Sam were falling together, crashing and tumbling over each other as the crows continued to flail at them.

They landed at the bottom with a mighty *snap*, and Sam's vision went black for a moment, just a moment, and when she opened her eyes she could see

Blue Charlie on the floor next to her, still grasping her ravaged arm.

The wooden man had suffered a massive, jagged crack at his neck from the fall, almost severing his head. The hand clippers were now buried to the hilt in his left eye.

His wooden lips opened and closed, labored, sluggish. Tiny blue roses bloomed on his head and chest and then wilted instantly, shriveling and turning black.

Finally, his mouth stopped moving and the roses stopped blooming, and she was certain that Blue Charlie had died.

The crows retreated, those that were still alive, scattering and disappearing up the stairwell and out the bathroom window, the battle won, and Sam's eyes fluttered, a dim and lovely warmth wrapping around her.

We've slept too long, she heard Charlie say from somewhere behind her, and she began to laugh, to cry, to weep, because it *was* his voice, the voice she had always fallen so hard for when he whispered or spoke or sang to her, and she turned to face him finally, her partner in crime 'til the end of time, her everything, the love of her life.

SOMATIC EMBRYOGENESIS

NO ROSE WITHOUT THE THORN

"No book is truly the work of just one author. I've had the privilege of leaning on many hands to help piece together this timeline, and I owe them all my deepest gratitude. From the bottom of my heart, thank you. But there is one person who stands apart, the one without whom this journey—this story—would never have come to fruition.

Samantha Perry. The love of my life. My partner in crime 'til the end of time. The one who has shared in every triumph, every setback, and every moment in between. Sam was not only the unwavering support behind the facts and the research, but also the photographer who captured the heart of this trip—the images, the moments, the details that made it all real. I could never have done this without her. More than that, I wouldn't have wanted to.

She is, in every way, the true captain of this ship, steering us through the stormy seas of our lives with a steady hand and a heart full of courage. I look ahead to whatever adventures await us, in this world and the next, with more excitement than I could ever express.

If, as I've often said, people are like the **thorns** of a rose—leaving their marks on us in ways both small and profound—then Sam has become a part of me in the deepest, most permanent sense. She is embedded in my heart and soul, a mark that will never fade.

As always, babydoll, this one is for you."

- Charles Perry,
No Rose Without the Thorn

Dawn broke.

At first glance, the house at the end of the street looked like any other house on the block, a late 60's modernist two story with an unkempt, vacant lot next to it.

But on closer inspection, one might notice how overgrown the property was – not by grass and weeds, but by tiny, shaggy, beautiful blue roses that wound their way not just through the lawn, but also climbed the fence and even the corners of the house.

On the second floor, a broken window, short and wide, most likely to a bathroom. Growing from that tiny black rectangle were more of the blue roses, climbing up the siding above the window and curling along the roof gutters.

Inside, the house was hushed except for the strange rustling noise coming from behind the walls, bristly vines sliding against thorny canes.

The blue roses spilled from heater grates and light fixtures, from electrical outlets and baseboard moldings.

Hundreds of dead crows littered the stairs, with the tiny carcasses so thick in places that they resembled black, feathery rugs. At the bottom of the staircase, only stains and smudges, broken feathers and broken branches, to ever suggest what had transpired.

The kitchen door opened onto a concrete patio, hidden by the canes and creeping, invasive vines of the massive blue rosebush that now dominated the small garden and threatened to overrun the entire backyard.

A large space had been cleared at the thick, thorny trunk of that bush, a lumpy, muddy mess of disturbed ground, littered with snapped rose canes and torn, celeste blue petals. A tiny garden sign had been jammed into the dirt, listing drastically.

Collapsed on the patio in front of the garden, Samantha's body. She was motionless on the bed of thorns she laid upon.

Her arms were filthy, ruined, caked to the elbows with mud and blood. She was unconscious, sleeping like the dead.

The weak glow of dawn cut the sky, breaking through the towering rosebush and into the yard, inching up her battered but peaceful face. As it reached her eyelids, she stirred.

She sat up slowly, painfully, yawning and reaching one hand up to the pink and orange sky, mesmerized by the sunlight that slipped between her torn and muddy fingers.

She turned to face the garden.

There, bursting from the packed dirt in front of the rosebush was a gnarled, thorny forearm ending in a twisted, wooden hand, its fingers wrapped around a solitary rose cane, as if presenting a gift.

And blooming from that single, bristly stem was a brilliant, sky-blue rose.

Samantha's face lit up and she crawled to the hand, stroking it, cradling it in her own.

The wooden fingers began to twitch.

The little girl's voice that spilled from Samantha's lips said only one, ecstatic word.

"Daddy!"

Author's Note

Grief is a funny thing. Not "funny ha-ha," of course, but in the way it sneaks up on us and leaves us gutted, even though it's the one universal experience we all share. It's remarkable, really, that we humans - who know full well that death is inevitable - can still be so profoundly derailed by it. Every single person on this planet will face it, and yet, when it happens, it hits us like a total surprise. Scientists estimate that 109 billion people have lived and died on Earth - billions of lives that ended before ours - and still, we're stunned when someone we love catches the last train out. If that's not a flaw in our emotional wiring, I don't know what is.

We've all either known someone - or been that someone - who reacts to loss like Samantha Perry. When someone you love dies, there's a part of you that tries to bargain with The Universe. You make deals with God, the Devil, or whatever higher power you may believe in. When that fails, you cling to the comforting idea that the person you lost is still around in some way, watching over you, and how fucking awful for them would that be if it were true? Imagine having an afterlife only to spend it watching your kid or your sibling or your partner slog through the day at school or a job they hate and then doom-scroll on Instagram all night.

Now, what if - after all that grieving and bargaining - you thought you *did* get them back? You'd put up with a lot of horrible shit, I bet. I mean, I bet *I* would. I used to joke that I wanted to die early because I thought I wouldn't be able to handle the pain of losing the people I loved. Turns out I was right.

Like my previous books, **Thorns** started life as a screenplay. I originally wrote it for my good friend Wade Chitwood to direct. The movie never happened, but I'm thrilled that Wade agreed to supply the cover and illustrations for this book. He's an incredible artist and, like me, has turned to adapting his screenplays into novels. Dig his work. It's worth your time.

I also owe a huge thanks to my friend Meredith Hewett for helping me with the photography jargon in the story. If anything sounds a little off, that's on me for tweaking it to fit the narrative.

Finally, take a moment to hug the people you care about while you can. You won't regret the time you took to let someone know you loved them.

kly
11/22/22 - 12/15/24

"THORNS" production sketch by John Fulton, 2019

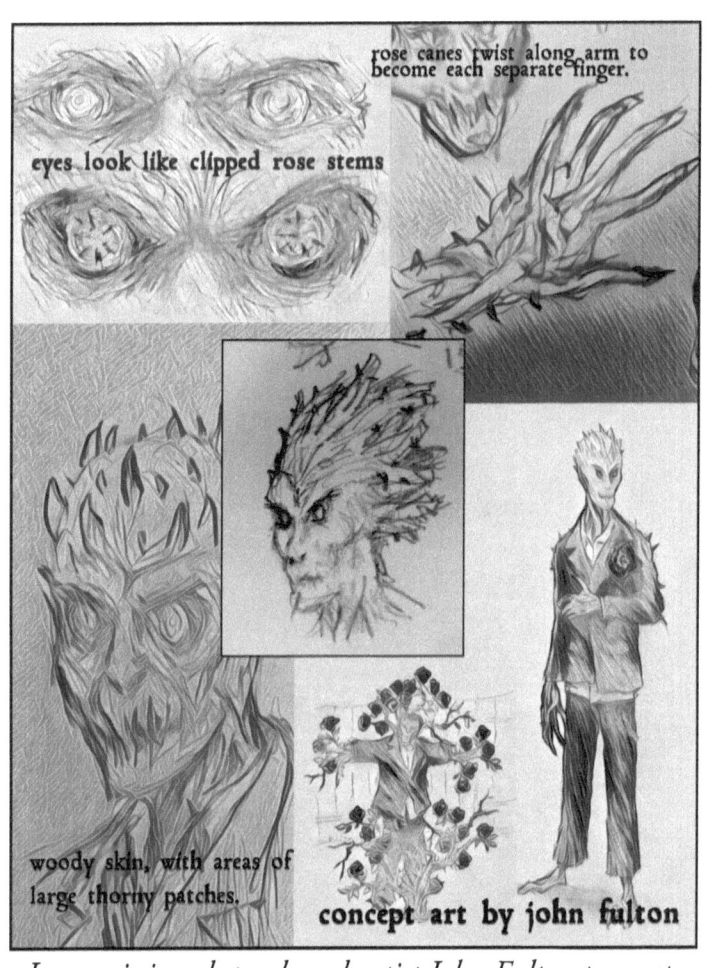

rose canes twist along arm to become each separate finger.

eyes look like clipped rose stems

woody skin, with areas of large thorny patches.

concept art by john fulton

I commissioned storyboard artist John Fulton to create some production sketches which I included in the final script when I delivered it to Wade Chitwood. Circa May, 2019.

I had secretly taken photos of Wade's house and instructed John Fulton to use it in his production sketches. May, 2019

K.L. Young is an award-winning
filmmaker, publisher, and podcaster.
He lives in a pop-culture museum in
Washington State.